THE THIRD BOAT

Leila Mackinlay

A FIVE STAR PAPERBACK

Acknowledgements

To Messrs. Chatto and Windus Ltd. together with the executors of the late Hall Caine for permission to reproduce the passage from *The Shadow of a Crime* in Part 2 (I).

To the Royal National Life-Boat Institution for information regarding rescues off the Isle of Man.

To Miss A. Harrison, Librarian Archivist to the Manx Museum for advice; Miss I. M. Killip, Folk Life Survey Assistant to the above for reading the proof.

Also to the Manx Sailing and Cruising Club (the trophy mentioned as Ellan Vannin is imaginary). The lifeboat report used in connection with the yachting incident took place on August 5th, 1965, but not, of course, with the same people or cruiser.

❁

Bibliography
Lancashire Plain and Seaboard, Herbert Collins (Dents) in Part I.

And for those sections laid in the Isle of Man:
Ward Lock's Red Guide.
Portrait of the Isle of Man by C. H. Stenning (Hale).
The Isle of Man by S. P. B. Mais (Christopher Johnson).

❁

This edition published in MCMLXXII by
PBS Limited, Victoria Mills, Pollard Street,
Manchester M4 7AU

Made and printed in Great Britain by
C. Nicholls & Company Ltd
The Philips Park Press, Manchester

THE THIRD BOAT

Author's Note

In this novel I have attempted to show how elements of tragedy may run through the lives of certain families over several generations. Though the setting is contemporary, plot and situations being pure invention, the historical incidents recalled are factual and based upon authentic material. The characters concerned, however, are imaginary.

There is, of course, a Harry Kelly's Cottage at Creigneish, and there seemed little point in making it someone else's. In the same way I have used typical Manx names, familiar there as the Murphys or O'Connors in Ireland, but there is no intention of referring to anyone with the same names. My excuse for having used them is that they help to establish the setting.

L.M.
London 1965-6.

Part 1
LAVINIA CUSHING

'What a magnificent portrait! Who is she?'

The picture in question had drawn me irresistibly across the room to stare, in sheer wonderment. The young woman was vibrantly, exultantly alive, from the challenge in those clear, well-spaced eyes to the lift of the arrogant chin. Her dress, an exquisitely muted cerese, put the period as somewhere around the 1850's; too late to have been a Gainsborough which the 'following' effect of the eyes suggested. If I were a little out in my dates it might just conceivably have been a very late Lawrence, though the style did not suggest this.

My host came and stood beside me, saying in a reflective voice. 'I agree that it's a strangely arresting picture. Everyone who comes to the house seems drawn to it, as you have been.'

'You haven't answered my question yet, Sir Justin. Who *is* the nineteenth century lovely? An ancestor of yours, perhaps?'

Sir Justin Hardcastle shook his head. Unromantically, he feared, the portrait had been taken over with the house. The previous owners had left Cartmel for a flat in Grange-over-Sands itself, which necessitated the selling off of various possessions: furniture, glass and one or two paintings too big—they opined—for a modern flat.

'I must confess my surprise that they let this particular picture go.' In size it was only what, I believe, is called Kitcat dimensions. 'Not that it has any intrinsic value,' he went on 'The artist is practically unknown. Just a local. Not even an R.A.'

'Anyone who could depict such miraculous "life" on a canvas deserves recognition.'

Sir Justin agreed. 'As a matter of fact I made it my business to find out what I could both about the artist—and his sitter. Perhaps you would care to hear Lavinia Cushing's story?'

'Lavinia Cushing,' I mouthed the name experimentally, deciding that it did not really suit her. A bit too dull and decorous, but of those times. For myself I would have preferred Rosanna.

'You writers are all the same, Wickham. Out for copy,' Sir Justin teazed, fetching drinks which he set upon an exquisite Chippendale coffee table. Had that, too, gone with the house? He lived in one of those charming Georgian places which toned so well in this ancient spot, with its one-time Augustinian Priory of which the Norman church with its lovely old glass, the memorials and tombs happily remained.

Knowing that I proposed to see the Lake District Sir Justin, an acquaintance of my father's, had very kindly suggested spending a few days with him first in Cartmel, which proved a delightful centre; within reach of the Fells and the pleasant seaside resort of Grange. As a stranger I had made the initial mistake of bathing in the open sea instead of using the swimming pool and quickly found treacherous currents and shifting sands which, to a weaker swimmer, could have proved very dangerous indeed.

It was about the Sands that Sir Justin now began to talk. In order to understand the Cushing story it was necessary, he said, to make me familiar with certain local phenomena.

'You may have heard that—given the right conditions—it is possible to cross Morecambe Bay via the Sands? The old route ran from Hest Bank to Kent Bank, then over land through Flookburgh for the second crossing between Conishead Priory and Bardsea. The final Channel was the Keer one.'

He implied that a great deal of romantic nonsense had been written upon the subject of ghostly visions of coaches plunging to their doom.

'The whinny of horses and the screams of drowning men. Oh, people drowned all right. According to Cartmel registers, one hundred and forty one of them between fifteen fifty-nine and eighteen-eighty, but that is only *one* record. Others may— or may not exist. You see when there happens to be a sea mist or heavy fog, the whole area can become featureless as a desert. Not a known landmark will remain. Think how easily a man could be lost! Death from drowning becomes all but inevitable and the bodies would show up when the tide went out. In fact there used to be a local saying that old so and so hadn't died in bed, but "in th' sands".'

'Since the undertaking was so hazardous why did people do it?'

The reason was practical: until the coming of the Ulverston-Lancaster railway in eighteen fifty-seven—the coach at a fare of five shillings—had been the shortest route.

'By road via Kendal meant forty miles. Maybe you'll have seen the stones built into the wall at Headless Cross stating that Lancaster was fifteen miles over the sands? Even when the New Turn-pike was opened—in eighteen twenty—it still meant thirty-four miles whereas the shore route was only twenty, all told.'

One began to see the reason for the popularity—especially in the days of horse-drawn vehicles.

My curiosity about Lavinia Cushing was not to be satisfied just yet, for Sir Justin was something of an authority on the history of 'the sands' and not to be hurried. He spoke well and interestingly about them and I began to see that his peroration was necessary. The finer points of the tragic story could not have been appreciated until the general background had been adequately sketched-in for my benefit.

Back in the 1820's, then, Hest Bank had its pier and was a key point for the transporting on of goods intended for Kendal and Lancaster, across Morcambe Bay sands. There was a regular stage coach service from the King's Arms or the Bear and Staff in Lancaster crossing the river to Skerton to reach Hest Bank, where the hotel had a room which displayed a lighted lantern from sundown.

'To guide the late traveller on to the sands.'

The crossing was safe only at specific times; during the four-hour period of ebb-tide or the two-hour one when it was incoming. In all, a safety margin of only six hours. Sir Justin read me a report made by a certain Dickson, writing graphically indeed about the number of unfortunates lost annually *crossing these deceitful sands.* It did, he stated, touch *the nerve of humanity.*

'We have already spoken of the danger from mist—often heavy in these parts, as you know from personal experience, Wickham. The risk was as bad for anyone caught by the incoming tide.'

Mr. Dickson also mentioned the three river fords—namely Kent, Keer and Leven—which lay on the route. Their exact position might not be familiar to the traveller and vessels could cause holes in the sands.

'Keer Channel is roughly two miles out from Hest Bank. Until eighteen-twenty I'm afraid it was left to coach drivers to select their crossing point. Subsequently proper guides become compulsory.'

Even that, it appeared, did not entirely rule out mishap. After Keer there were some four miles overland before the Kent Channel, which was considered easy, 'deep, changing and swift flowing' though it was.

From then the olden times journey proceeded ahead for the Guide's House, close to Kent's Bank.

'This was not a difficult undertaking either.' Overland to Flookburgh or—later, Cark also—thence to Sandgate, formerly Sand Road, where there was the next crossing.

'At one time the further shore was gained between Conishead Priory and Bardsea: later, one which led to the Guide's House at Ulverston.'

Sir Justin showed me a sketch map which clarified things and indicated how comparatively wide the fords were. 'You can only cross Keer Channel,' indicating this with his forefinger. 'Three hours after ebb.'

He went on to produce an account by 18th century John Lucas who gave a graphic picture of what are quite obviously quicksands in places. A little before rain one was reputed to hear: *a hissing Noise, occasioned by the breathing of innumerable little Bubbles, and will feel a noysom stinking savour.*

He took the reason for this phenomena to be: *that the Pores of the Sand as well as of the Earth, are at such times unlock'd*

Sir Justin and I exchanged smiles at this artless yet somehow charming theory. 'Streams of crude sulphur' mixed—most unpleasantly one gathers—with 'salts'. This effluvia appeared to have been a sure sign of rain.

'There is evidence of a quicksand "Pool" and a compass would be an essential for even remotely safe navigation.'

When the carters followed this regular route one of their number would start out at ebb tide, mounted upon a white horse for clearer visibility, as did the later official guides.

'The path would be marked with branches by a process known as "brodding" or "brobbing" which is testing by pole, to discover a firm bottom to the sea-bed. Local fishers still carry on this tradition. Your carter then blew loudly upon his horn and remained in position till the flood time commenced. A second blast of sound and he returned to shore. According to Lucas, the Kent ran with incredible swiftness and was full of mud, its width at the fording point being dangerous because the state of the river bed was so uncertain. Fair one day, hopeless the next. The actual quicksands—he calls them "Syrtes"—and the "Poos" (or rivulets) could be detected by the smoothness and their overall shine.'

On reflection this was something the way it had been during my bathe over at Grange which, had I known more then, I might not have essayed, little though I cared for swimming pools.

Even the name of Grange-over-Sands bore out the truth (later confirmed by Sir Justin) of the name's derivation, for until the middle of the 19th century the only approach remained across the sands. The Channels constantly moved and the old river bed would appear at its worst when not fully sanded; only wet.

'What they call a "Lyring". Sometimes there can be other conditions. The stream may throw up high sandbanks but continue to undermine them, so that the sand falls noisily into the river: Great slabs of it, Wickham. Yes, indeed, as the old saw runs, "The Kent and the Keer have parted many good man and his meear".'

Meear I took to mean wife, but might well have been incorrect.

'Despite the conditions I've outlined to you, people crossed in the course of daily business. The earliest coaches on the routes were diligences. Popularly known as "the dillies"—just as we in our day talk of tubes and buses,' and he laughed, pausing only to take another sip of whisky and soda.

Mrs. Gaskell, he went on, writing in 1858, described how she had looked down upon Morecambe Bay: *With its slow moving train of crossers, led over the treacherous sands by the Guide, a square man sitting stern on his horse.*

And not above—if the good lady is to be believed—leaving people to their probable fate by drowning if unprepared to pay his fee.

'The sound of that ram's horn being blown from across the sands must have been an eerie signal,' mused Sir Justin. Then: 'You have hidden your impatience well! I promise to reach Lavinia Cushing in a moment. First, this,' he handed me a list of disasters as compiled by one William Stout. It made terrible reading.

In 1821—loss of one postchaise quite close to Hest Bank. The occupant, post boy and horse—all drowned. Both in 1825 and 1828 the Lancaster-Ulverston coach had succumbed. Blown over, during a storm in the first instance, passengers being rescued but the horse drowned. On the second occasion the vehicle simply sank into the sands, the passengers scrambling free but no mention of the horse. In 1846 nine young folk home-

16

bound for Cartmel after Ulverston Whitsuntide Fair were also —as Sir Justin put it—'sacrificed to the sands'.

'It is understood that the cart simply disappeared into a water hole and that the travellers following on behind never heard a sound.'

'Good God!'

The last account related to 1857 when seven farm hands bound for the hiring fair were likewise drowned.

'A terrible record, as you must agree, Wickham.'

'And was Lavinia Cushing another victim?'

His lean, intellectual face became mildly disapproving. I was made to feel like an inattentive schoolboy instead of an author who had enjoyed some small success since giving up schoolmastering in order to become a whole-time writer. A not inconsiderable decision in one's thirties but then I was still a bachelor and therefore free to take the risk.

'Lavinia came of good yeoman stock. Her father was a local fisherman; the wife had been in service before her marriage. There were two daughters. Lavinia, the elder and her sister, Charlotte.'

'But she looks as though she were of aristocratic parentage!' My protest was almost involuntary and my eyes were again on the portrait. A fisherman's child? With *that* bearing?

Sir Justin shrugged philosophically.

'Cushing made a decent enough living by his nets, I dare say. In any case, in the days before the railway existed—I'm unable to give you the precise date for the story but with your pertinacity you could doubtless find out!'

I nodded, fully intending at any rate to try.

'The Cushing family set out across the sands. For what purpose, we are not told. Maybe to visit somebody or to attend a fair. If it had been a simple fishing expedition I doubt the necessity for the women-folk's presence. On their way they were suddenly overtaken by one of the sea frets I have mentioned. The sands were virtually obliterated. Cushing stopped the cart—quite near one of the river banks probably—and after

17

discussion with his family, no doubt, decided that the best thing he could do was to explore the way ahead. Possibly he might be fortunate enough to meet someone who would guide the family onwards.'

It must be assumed that Cushing would have known the sands' route well enough. He must have crossed by them on many a previous occasion. On this particular one there were the lives of his wife and daughters to be taken into account as well as his own. In my mind's eye I could picture this man moving into the damp, clinging curtain of mist; vainly searching for landmarks which would assist him in locating his position. Even the cart itself would be difficult to see, once he had left it.

'Cushing had not returned by the tide-change,' Sir Justin went on. 'The predicament of those in the cart would be very real. And how great their anxiety, for unless he had had quite amazing luck—or fog had dispersed beyond their range of vision—the chances of his survival must have seemed almost nil.'

Despite the warmth of the room, with its shutters closed and a small electric stove keeping a pleasant temperature, I found myself shivering.

'We may imagine that the two daughters would do their best to counsel a return the way they had come. At least that made sense, but Mrs. Cushing refused to leave the cart, arguing that her husband might even yet return. The girls stayed with her, comforting her, trying to keep alive hope in despondency. They remained as long as they could.'

'And then?'

'Maybe the mother begged them to save themselves, or maybe they just went.'

'How exactly?'

'According to the story the girls rode back to the shore and when their horse was drowned, swam for it.'

'They were both saved?'

Sir Justin nodded. 'The end of the story is very sad. Cushing either wandered around in circles and ended up in the spot where he first started or else went ahead and then turned back again; hopeless of finding any way forward. At all events the bodies were found at the next ebb tide. Husband and wife, quite close to one another. And, further away still, the horse. All three dead ' "i' th' sands".'

Sympathetic though I was bound to feel for the Cushing couple and their faithful dobbin, my main interest was still with Lavinia. Could Sir Justin carry the story forward at all from that point? Or did it end, as it had begun, in the Bay?

'Records are scrappy,' he admitted. 'Charlotte remained around Leven. For sentimental reasons? Who shall say. I imagine that she will have married; perhaps a fisherman, like her father.'

'Lavinia?' I prompted, unwilling to consign this glorious young woman to a future among nets and lobster pots.

'Oh, Lavinia left Lancashire. Possibly the memories of this place were too poignant to be borne. More probably—and I'm sure you'll agree with this theory, Wickham—she was ambitious. With her looks she doubtless sought to better herself. There is evidence of her leaving for London.'

At this juncture theories had to take the place of corroborated facts. It was not known what she did when she reached the capital. Possibly she went into service.

'Be that as it may, Wickham, she made a good marriage. All the things, I suppose, an attractive young woman of the times would want. House in London. Attentive but not too demanding husband. Fine clothes and jewels. A carriage and pair in place of the Cushing cart or the "dilly". Happiness, you may think, does not exist in material things alone. Perhaps Lavinia wearied of the social life and longed for the freedom of the Fells. Or she may have thought too long had passed without seeing her sister, Charlotte. At all events Lavinia came back to Bardsea village. And there she met Ambrose Keeling, the fellow who did that,' nodding towards the picture.

There was no need to tell me that Keeling must have fallen

in love with his sitter. How else could he have painted as divinely as he had?

Sir Justin smiled. 'I can see that you are one step ahead of me! You are right, of course. They fell in love. There was a brief, heady romance at which Charlotte possibly connived. Lavinia's absence from home lengthened and her husband grew suspicious. Gossip can travel immense distances or he may have known his Lavinia.'

I could accept a love affair as between a struggling young artist—most artists *do* struggle at some stage of their career—and the fisherman's daughter who bettered herself, but not the implication that she was just a wife of easy virtue. The eyes were too candid. What if the lips appeared a little full? It was a proud rather than a sensual mouth!

The husband came. Had he put up perhaps at one of those Greenodd inns, opened once all day and full of seafarers? Or had he gone further down the estuary to Ulverston. Either would have been near—yet not too near.

'The lovers, alerted, planned to elope together but Lavinia's husband, one Francis Davage, prevented their escape.'

'How?' I asked, unbelievably anxious.

'He carried a duelling pistol, threatening to shoot the artist but Lavinia flung herself on her husband. And the pistol went off, whether accidentally or not, it was impossible to tell. Lavinia was mortally wounded.'

That was almost the end of the story. Davage stood trial but was acquitted. It could only have been upon a charge of manslaughter. The artist disappeared from the district. Little was known of his subsequent paintings—assuming there were any, but if he never again placed brush to canvas he had left at least one exquisite example of his talent in the portrait of Lavinia Cushing.

2

It had been a long talking session and my host looked tired so shortly afterwards I went up to my room. Once in bed I found it difficult to sleep and a book which normally should have held my attention failed to interest me. I read and re-read the same passage, taking nothing in so gave up the attempt and switched out the bedside light. There was a clear, star-filled sky outside and the gentlest of breeze to stir the drawn-aside curtains. (To sleep in darkness is anathema to me.) The only dissonance was created by local youths who rode their motor bikes round and round the square as if it were a circus ring.

In Lavinia Cushing's time there was probably only the hooting of an owl.

Strange how the tale had affected me. As is my habit I took myself over it again in stages, picturing to myself the horror of those sinking sands. Did people still make the journey? I had a vague idea that it might be retained, in modified form no doubt, as a tourist attraction and must remember to ask Sir Justin. It would be something to follow even a little way along the track which Lavinia had trod that night when she and her sister became orphans.

There must be something peculiarly frightening about not knowing whether the next step forward would be on to firm sand or whether it would simply give, and suck you down into it. My personal experience of quicksands was somewhat limited. I recalled them at Burnham-on-Sea in Somerset where bathing times were strictly high tide: oozy, clayey mud was not necessarily the same thing.

Lavinia must have been a goodish swimmer. Her sister, too. In fancy I tried to picture them reluctant surely still to leave their mother to her lonely vigil in the cart. What ages were the girls at the time? How tantalising not to know!

What must they have felt on the following day when their parents were found? Would the emotion of personal relief in survival have been mingled with natural sorrow? (Like it or not, self-preservation is probably the most powerful of all human instincts.)

Left alone, how had the girls existed? Had relatives or sympathetic villagers seen to their well-being? Tantalising indeed to have so many questions never to be answered.

My thought-trend shifted from Bardsea to London. Imagination could invent the situations in which Lavinia may have found herself but, at best they remain speculative. Had Francis Davage fancied her as she served him, caught glimpse of her at the playhouse or rode in Rotten Row and observed her among the crowd? Above all what sort of a man was he, apart from being rich?

I did not care to consider her as property of a licentious Corinthian, or of a man who was frequently in his cups. The marriage can scarcely have been a love match—at least upon her side.

Then there was the artist fellow: Ambrose Keeling. Him I pictured as young, impressionable, a little Keatsian. Had they climbed the Fells together; walked round Cartmel itself, maybe, as I had been doing these past few days?

Not the sands. Surely never again on the sands....

Imagination even supplied the final scene, set in some house where the lovers lived together. The irate and threatening husband, brandishing his duelling pistol and calling the artist vile names. Ambrose perhaps trying to be brave, if only for the sake of Lavinia. How the two men really looked, of course, I had not the slightest idea but the casting director who lives within every author had the artist tall and slender, though as a fellsman he may equally have been sturdy and short of stature. Davage was rubicund, bellicose, with pale, angry eyes and hair that tended to be ginger.

'I'll teach you to make love to my wife, you insolent young scoundrel!'

22

Lavinia, because I knew exactly how she really had looked, confronted her husband, scornful, unrepentant, chin raised just as it was in the picture. Then crack! The spurt of flame and Lavinia sinking at her lover's feet, with Davage—dazed, I hope—regarding her.

An idea struck me. She might be buried in the district. (It was unlikely that Davage had had her body removed to some family sepulchre of his own.) I would commence searching the local graveyards on the morrow. This would provide an interesting *raison d'etre* for my walks, upon which resolution I fortunately dropped asleep.

Sir Justin greeted me courteously at breakfast. His wife, who was almost as charming as himself, was behind the coffee and the tea.

'Good morning, Mr. Wickham. I'm afraid my husband kept you up late with his story-telling.'

'An engrossing evening, Lady Hardcastle.'

She smiled, claiming to have heard the Cushing story often enough for it to have lost its novelty.

'Since you are so interested, you may care to take a pilgrimage to her grave'—the word "pilgrimage" carried a slight, humorous stress. 'She's actually buried in Bardsea, I believe. It's a pretty village, if you haven't been there. It's too far to walk from here, of course, but I'm sure Sir Justin will be pleased to drive you over.'

I thanked them both for making my intention feasible. Since it was a comparatively fine morning, though rain clouds undoubtedly threatened to disburse their contents before the afternoon, we went directly after breakfast, leaving Lady Hardcastle to whatever it was she had to do around Cartmel.

'Kate'—the nickname was almost inevitable and a tribute to Goldsmith—'hasn't much of a stomach for cemeteries,' Sir Justin spoke lightly as we set off in his car; a good hill-climber but not a very recent model. Flash cars seemed to go with city-life in the country there were mostly dependable oldies, either shockingly shabby or as carefully preserved as this one was.

23

On the drive we discussed the—to me, at least—fascinating question of the way in which tragedy ran in families. From the Hapsburgs with their Mayerling, via the fated Romanovs of Russia and the wretched Emperor Maximillian of Mexico with his mad wife and martyr's end for himself, we were back again with the Cushings. It could be argued, Sir Justin was saying, that the disaster on the night of the sea-mist was 'suffering enough' for any one family, without the subsequent shooting of Lavinia.

'There was no—no issue to the Davage marriage?'

'None that I know of,' he answered. 'Of course Charlotte may have had children. The Parish register, if it goes back far enough, might help you there.'

Neither of us stopped to recall that we did not know for certain that Charlotte ever had married: much less what her name might have become. Still information on the Cushings in general could prove worth the research—though what use to me the material ultimately would be, I had not yet thought. Always below the present book upon which an author may be engaged at any given time was apt to germinate the idea for his next.

Not that I had any conscious intentions regarding the Cushings. My immediate plans were quite other. The educational publishers for whom I had written a modern textbook for school use on the period of literature known as 'Chaucer to the Jacobeans' were anxious to issue a re-evaluation of Hall Caine as a writer. Why, since his books are as little read today as Marie Corelli's, is difficult to see. However the job was mine for the doing, so to speak. A visit to the Isle of Man, which I scarcely knew, would become imperative at some stage in the writing but for the moment it was the Lake district for me, after Cartmel, then back to town to finish my sixth novel in time for the autumn date-line.

'Fate is a curious thing,' Sir Justin was observing, as we joined the A590, which we would be leaving after Ulverston to drop down into Bardsea via the A5087 coastal road. 'Some families seem to be dogged by the most appalling bad luck while others, amongst which I'm happy to include my own, seem to jog along more or less happily. Or at least no great dramatic event can be instanced that will make them in any way different from hundreds of others. One can't escape the natural cycle of birth and death, of course, but it is not part of the Almighty's plan, apparently, that there has to be violence and danger in addition.'

'You would exclude war as an example of private fate '

'Wouldn't you? It seems to me that war is of itself so colossal —so catastrophic, that it affects the lives of whole nations, not just individuals.'

I found myself thinking back over my own family without recalling abnormally dramatic events suggesting that we were pursued by *Hubris*. Most Wickhams die in their beds. We were distinguished by neither murder nor mayhem. True there had been a taint of mild mental disorder on my mother's side, but way back in early Victorian days. Deaths in childbirth I was inclined to dismiss—as Sir Justin would—as natural events of which most families doubtless had their quota.

'One asks oneself why perfectly simple fisherfolk should have been singled out for high drama in this way. Did Cushing take an undue risk in leading his family on to the sands on that particular day?' Sir Justin sounded his hooter twice at a half-asleep hiker who nipped nimbly aside as we passed to receive my host's ironic salute of 'thank you'.

'We must assume they had good reason to go. That the mist was not threatening when they started, or presumably they would never have done so. Any fisherman who uses these sands comes to know them intimately.'

Our argument shifted slightly as to what extent man might be said to control his personal fate. Said my host, in conclusion:

'The odd thing as I see it, Wickham, is the precise *purpose* why Lavinia Cushing was spared from drowning only to meet a still more violent form of death in the end.'

25

The sort of question to which there never could be a satisfactory answer.

It might have been pleasurable to walk from the outskirts of Ulverston, via Conishead Priory, and so down into Bardsea village, however since my host did not suggest leaving the car—few drivers ever do—it was hardly my place to do so.

The beginning was not exciting; just one of those modern overspills of uninteresting houses, and Bardsea Hall was no more than a ruin.

'A family of that name used to live there,' Sir Justin informed me. 'Received a grant of land not long after the Conquest, I believe. The line appears to have ended at Nicholas de Bardsey of Jacobean days.'

Old limestone cottages in the village street were more cheering but the church was modern: 1843. Still its crown-of-the-hill position was impressive and I imagined the spire made a landmark seen for miles and miles. There was no question but it dominated the entire village.

We parked and went to investigate. True the newer stonework was thrown up against the mellowed and ancient stone of the houses.

'You'll notice how they crowd together to fend off the rough weather, Wickham.'

However the real ecclesiastical interest lay in the Urswick Church—three miles distant—and in the end that was where our search took us. Not only was there a Viking cross in the North wall of the chancel but a long line of vicars dating back to Daniel le Fleming A.D. 1150-60. There were also fascinating tithe regulations and data about parish apprentices put out to work by 18th century Poor Law overseers. Vagrancy received a very curt reception: 'Its relief being deemed not an act of charity, but *Encouragement to laziness and vice.*

'I must show you the remains of the cock fighting ring on the Green before we leave,' said Sir Justin, 'but meanwhile—hadn't we better have a look for Lavinia Davage's grave?'

26

After a little wandering we found the tombstone for which we were looking.

It was standing out-of-true in the way that very old stones will, when the level of ground has shifted. No one had tended or cared for Lavinia's last resting place for many years. The grass was just about scythed, that was all. The wording on the stone was none too easy to read. She was born in the April of 1841 so assuming that the incident of the sands was sometime around '57 or a little earlier, she must have been sixteen or thereabouts when she swam for safety, and only thirty-one when she died.

'Passing sweet are the domains
of tender memory.'

A charming epitaph. Wordsworth, unless I was very much mistaken. (It turned out to be an extract from his *Ode to Lycoris*). On impulse I exclaimed:

'I wonder who selected the words? Charlotte or Davage?'

The thought was intriguing. Had it been the idea of the surviving Cushing sister, filled with love for her poor dead Lavinia?

Sir Justin plumped for the widower; it would have been a typically Victorian gesture.

'Even though he shot her?' my tone must have sounded somewhat astringent.

'Remember, Wickham, that shooting *may* have been an accident. I feel Wordsworth a bit erudite for a fisherman's daughter.'

'Unless she, too, had done better for herself.'

He shrugged. 'As you say.'

I could see he was bored and in any case the expedition had taken us rather longer than expected.

'Shall we go then, Wickham? My wife dislikes unpunctuality at mealtimes.'

On the return drive we talked of quite different topics.

No agreed limit had been set me for the stay in Cartmel but

27

I felt it time to move on; as the proverb has it 'Fish and guests smell at three days old', and already I had been with the Hard-castles for five. They were infinitely courteous but did not try to dissuade me, aware that plans—even nebulous as mine—were meant to be carried out. So, after a final private look at the portrait of the ill-fated red-head Lavinia, I made my way up towards the Lakeland proper.

Unfortunately it had not been possible to arrange a trip across even part of the Morecambe Bay sands. This 'attrac-tion' was strictly tourist-seasonal, which my visit was not. No local guide was willing to take me, even for a consideration and the trip was one I could hardly venture upon alone, having no wish to die 'i' th' sands'. Doubtless it was not all that danger-ous at the present day and Sir Justin had told me that the three-ford crossings of that old twenty-mile walk were no longer attempted. In adverse conditions the Guides would not set out at all, whatever the private diappointment of their sen-sation-seeking clients. So I contented myself with a brief saun-ter, close to the shore, trying to stimulate my imagination into recapturing the past. But it was difficult, with a rare glint of sunshine and the distractions of playing children and barking dogs. Kicking a piece of orange peel angrily aside, I gave up the attempt ...

This might be a convenient moment to add a few relevant details about myself. By birth a north countryman I had nevertheless drifted south, though the bleaker, more bracing climate of my native moorlands would always suit me best and I returned to them, from time to time. My retired father had been a lecturer in Economics which accounted for my own start in the teaching profession. He still lived in our old home which I should be visiting before returning to London. Mother was a doctor's daughter, a gay and practical person with an enquiring mind it seemed her son had inherited.

My breakaway had come about quite naturally after college when I went to take up my first school appointment. I had liked the life but not well enough to want it for always. Being on the staff of a boys' public school was somewhat limiting; not so much as regards opportunity—a headmastership might come one's way provided one fitted requirements at a given time and did nothing upsetting to the Establishment. The constrictions were mental, rather than physical. Unless a man were careful he could develop into a kind of permanent prefect-type, his life interests encompassed by the quadrangle and his intellect never developing upon more adult lines. I had seen it happen all too often. With thirty in sight, I asked myself did I really wish to teach all my life? In a world rapidly becoming more and more bewilderingly scientific were not the classical studies I had been pounding into the often un-receptive heads of too many boys becoming outmoded?

Of course I could have tried my luck in the 'Blackboard Jungle' of a secondary modern or a comprehensive school in place of my over traditionalized public one. The brutal truth was that I did not care *enough* so when the textbook, happily compiled during our lengthy vacation periods began to 'go' I gave in my term's notice. Private cramming or holiday tutoring were available, if one wished. There was also examining work or the more prosaic duties of correcting 'scripts' for the G.C.E. and other examinations. All ways where money might be earned for limited periods of the academic year. Nowadays I used these sidelines less and less for truth to tell, living-in school had enabled me to put-by. While agreed that teaching salaries are far from adequate, posts including 'free board and lodge' give resident masters financial advantages over his day-school colleagues.

My first novel, largely autobiographical I fear, dealt with the world I knew best at that time. Then, artistically for a short time I had grown more adventuresome, seeking as it were the style of story to suit me. But now with my fifth and sixth books behind me I settled down into straight-forward narratives about modern themes ...

Mounted upon the cycle hired in Kendal and exploring the

lovely Lakeland area both on wheels and on foot, my restless mind might well have asked the question: 'Are you so sure the experimental novel-writing days really *are* over?' The hint, of course, was that I should break into the historical field and do what I could for Lavinia Cushing.

But enough of such follies!

I would be better employed to commence my studies on Hall Caine: 'Vigorous Christian Socialist'. *The Deemster, The Christian, The Eternal City, The Woman Thou Gavest Me,* etc. It was that little 'etc.' which daunted me! Caine was a writer of prodigious length and seriousness without, one suspected, the unintended humours which made Marie Corelli not bad reading even today. That Caine had been friend of D. G. Rossetti and his guest for many years was a fact to lead me from the main subject.

'A book confined to a re-evaluation of an out-of-fashion novelist is not enough on its own,' had been my attitude with the prospective publishers. 'I must be allowed to include his circle and to write-in the Manx background which influenced his entire choice of subject-matter.'

'It's your book, Jake.'

And on that satisfactory note I had been given what amounted to a roving commission and 'something in advance'.

There is no need to dwell upon my Lakeland holiday during which I was soaked on a number of occasions and at others enjoyed brief snatches of good weather. The Wickham homestead was between Harrogate and Blubberhouses, (a name which still afforded me rich humour) 'set amid fine moorland scenery' as one gazetteer described it. After the gracious Georgian home of the Hardcastles and the quiet—except for traffic—of Cartmel itself, ours was a sturdy, well-built, unaesthetic-looking house on the outskirts of town.

'Jake darling!' my little mother greeted me with the usual flattering rapture before studying me for signs of ill-health and, for ought I know, depravity. She found me too thin and not nearly bronzed enough.

'There hasn't been the sun, Mother.'

'True.' She gave my cheek a gentle pat and said, 'Come in and say hullo to your father.'

He was a very tall man with a hint of scholarly stoop. We shook hands affectionately as he asked:

'Well, and how's London?'

'There's nought so good as home,' I answered, trying to recall just how the vernacular went.

'You've acquired a Southerner's accent,' Father was mildly critical.

'I dare say that's true.'

He shot his specs up on to his forehead in a well-recalled gesture. His very blue eyes, which had been passed on to me, were as alertly interested in life around him as ever they had been. As a boy I remembered him dark, only a little grey in places; now he was quite white which made him look older than he really was. In colouring I favoured Mother more with a fair skin, which nevertheless tanned well under appropriate conditions, and fair hair worn 'squarishly' with 'short back and sides'.

There was a great deal to talk about; there always was. They were flatteringly interested in my writing, though I always felt that my father would have preferred me to have remained a teacher. Mother had read my books—bless her—and seemed to have liked the last one best. What were my future plans? She listened politely, but I felt without genuine interest, to the Hall Caine project.

'I read *The Manxman* as a girl, but to tell the truth, Jake, I can't remember much about it.'

Neither apparently could Father.

'What about the next novel?' she went on, so flatteringly interested in the doings of her only son that he felt a rotter for having stayed away so long.

'I haven't decided on that yet. There's time enough, for I'll have to make a start on this Hall Caine project.'

'Will you go over to the Isle of Man at all?' cut in Father

31

and I said that was my intention. Since he knew it rather well he made some useful suggestions as to where to stay and what to see. 'At twenty, one counsels Douglas. At thirty—I'd say Peel or Port Erin.'.

'Somewhere quiet.' It was in my mind to hire a car for one or two days.

'We went to Ramsey when you were six,' Mother said. 'Do you remember anything about it, Jake?'

I thought really hard. There had been an immense wheel.

'That's at Laxey. The wheel was constructed by one John Casement to keep the lead mines free from water. I think I've still a guide to the island knocking around. You'd better take it with you.'

We looked up Laxey's wheel when we found the book in question and learned that it had been erected in 1854, being 227 feet in circumference. 250 gallons could be pumped to the minute and ascent made up the 95 steps on to a 75 ft.—from-the-ground platform. Gratuitously we further were told that the word Laxey was from the Scandinavian (as I was to find so much over there was) and meant literally 'salmon river'. *Today no salmon are to be found there.* Thus in one cruel sentence the chronicler removed hope of a catchment!

I thought I also remembered horse trams (Douglas) though it could well be that pictures of them were not unfamiliar on holiday postcards; my father had not been over to the island since the war. He began to consider it as a possible thought for the future.

'Though I expect it'll have changed. Places do, my boy.'

'Isn't it rather we who change?'

'That could well be.'

While I was with them Mother made it her business, as always, to discover whether or not I had a young lady in the offing.

'You're over thirty now, Jake. Isn't it time you thought of marriage?'

I shifted uneasily, as I always had, glibly protesting that I was perfectly happy as I was.

32

'But to be in rooms!' she shook her head.

It was practical and the years of community living had made me appreciate my own company. Presumably I could have shared a flat with some other man but one needed to be sure that such an arrangement would work. As it was I had a pleasant landlady who gave me an exceptionally large room, which was kept cleaned for me. There was an upstairs kitchenette, shared with 'the offices' between three of us—so far without acrimony. We had worked out a satisfactory rota and there was a good deal of eating out; breakfast being provided. Since I was often in at different times from the other users of the kitchen life was easy. If not what might be called a cook, I was not above trying out experiments, some good, some not. Restaurant food was apt to become monotonous—and expensive.

These thoughts were interrupted by Mother still waiting to know if I have not met someone I 'liked'.

Liked? Yes, of course. Several, in fact! However that was not of itself enough. There had been physical attractions on the side, as it were, which I did not propose to discuss and one rather near-miss in my second year of teaching. Grand romance? Certainly not. Sex—well, yes. Love? That I had not yet fully experienced. Not the sort of love that was capable of making me know that there was the one woman with whom I longed to spend the rest of my life.

Sharply I reminded myself that no sane man could fancy that he had seen a suggestion of his ideal in a portrait of someone who had lived close on a hundred years earlier; Lavinia Cushing—never, to me, Lavinia Davage. Just a picture and a name upon a tombstone.

3

There were always the same feelings of regret—on both sides—when the time came for me to say good-bye to my parents. That indefinable sense of reproach on their part: defenceless-ness on mine. My right to leave had never been questioned. Nor should it have been. And yet—in my heart there would be a wholly irrational guilt. This generally lasted me all the way back to London, airless after my native Yorkshire and smelling more abominably than ever of diesel. Even the house where I had my room could appear unwelcoming. This, too, I knew to be ridiculous for my landlady was always pleased to see her 'guests' back. Guests—one felt—was a more acceptable term to her than lodgers.

Number 183 Southurst Road was on the fringe of N.W.8 and N.W.6 and therefore accessible. The house itself was one of those red-brick Victorian efforts, with fussy balconies and porch, but the rooms were splendidly proportioned with lofty ceilings and, before the oil fired central heating had been in-stalled, horribly chill. Huge casement windows let in all the London light there might be.

Mrs. Trapper evidently heard my taxi and was in the hall before I could use my key, expressing the hope that I had enjoyed my trip. Bubbles, the lean faced London cat, twined around her legs and gave a mildly bored mew at me. 'Mrs. T', as we called her amongst ourselves, was the antithesis of the conventional landlady, being far too kind-of-heart, one would think, to make much of a profit.

The house was on a very extensive lease, freehold in all but name, as she liked to say, because at sixty-odd, which she must have been, anything that might happen *after* the next forty years was unlikely to be of interest. A widow's pension and some typing work which she took in (most helpful to me, of course) added to the letting of rooms and made life possible, if not luxurious for her.

'I expect you'll like a cup of tea, Mr. Wickham, come through when you're ready, won't you?'

This was a routine part of the 'welcome home' and having dumped my luggage and tidied up, I made my way to the ground floor back garden room, heavily furnished in outmoded style but somehow rather shabbily comfortable. The massive sideboard, bookcases, armchairs and pembroke table would have dwarfed a room of lesser proportions. On the mantelpiece were two bronzed Greek figures, wrestling with—could it have been minotaurs?—and between them a big but sweet-chiming clock.

Mrs. T questioned me about my holiday with flattering interest and I even found myself telling her Lavinia Cushing's story.

'What an exciting book that's going to make, Mr. Wickham,' she said at the finish.

For some stupid, wholly inexplicable reason, the assumption riled me.

'I haven't made up my mind to use it,' I answered, I hope not with sharpness.

Evidently I had, though, and could see it in her face. Mrs. T had the common layman's view of writers: namely, that everything seen or heard by them was bound to end up in a book. That to a large degree this was true, did not make it more pleasant. Neither did the fact that friends and acquaintances studied our work in the hope of finding recognisable portraits of themselves. When we did happen to include some facet of a particular person, he or she almost invariably missed the fact.

'I just thought the story interesting, Mrs. Trapper. Historical novels aren't my line, as you know.'

She supposed not, but remained unconvinced.

Despite my assurances to the contrary I did a little further research about the Cushings when admittedly I ought to have been better employed reading Hall Caine. A ramble around the shelves of Hampstead's new and, to the squares, startling public library, put me in contact with a small volume called *The Lancashire Fishing Tradition* by a reverend gentleman to whom local history was a hobby. It was quite a slim book and much of the information contained therein was devoted to descriptions of the varieties of fish to be found around the Lancashire coast and the best methods of catching them. There was, however, a chapter called 'The peculiarities of Morecambe Bay' with a praiseworthily succint account of the fishermen's traditional use of 'th' sands'. Then, to my delight, I found a resumé of the Cushing tragedy, much as Sir Justin had told it. As one guessed, they had not been far out from Kent's Bank when the fog descended. The distance the girls swam was not, perhaps, excessive for young women brought up on a sea-border and probably almost thrown into the waves as children, though sea-bathing as such, was not universally recognised as a popular pastime in those days. Still one assumed locals needed to know how to swim. The author did not carry on Lavinia's story, beyond saying that she had left the district but he did prove helpful with regard to Charlotte:

The younger daughter remained in the locality all her life marrying a Levens farmer called Goodheart. They had several children most of whom were faithful to the area. Charlotte lived to a ripe old age and the pleasure of watching her grand-children grow up around her.

I copied this paragraph and sent it to Sir Justin, saying that I thought he would be interested. Came the reply:

If, as I suspect, you would like me to do a little further research in the matter of the Cushings—for both our sakes, I confess to renewed interest—I will communicate with you again if I have any success.

Meanwhile he signed himself 'Cordially J.H.'
36

With a feeling of highest virtue I returned the reverend's book to the library and took out *The Deemster*, writing a card for *The Manxman* at the same time. Having read them in the skipping method one acquires in reviewing books, ready to turn back again to them later, I also began a little preliminary study of the topography of the Isle of Man soon filling my notebooks with a great deal of information. One could not tell, at that stage anyway, how much would be of use. The history and ceremonies of the Tynwald no doubt: also the origin of the three-legged coat of arms which intrigues so many holidaymakers. Leaving out a precise account of its heraldic composition, it was interesting to know that it dated back to sixteen hundred and sixty-eight and meant: 'whichever way you throw me I shall stand.'

The position of the Lieutenant Governor, the legislative Council and House of Keys I was prepared to make highly relevant: the first corresponding to the sovereign, the others to the House of Lords and Commons respectively. And since people usually liked information about animals I proposed to throw in the news that there were no foxes, snakes or toads and mighty few frogs. No nightingales or jays visited the island and even kingfishers were rare. And of course one durst not omit *felix cattus*: either those semi-tail-less pussies akin to East Asian varieties affectionately known as 'stumpies' or the minustail, ones, 'rumpies'. I had not realised that manx cats actually moved their hind legs together and *hopped*, rabbit fashion! One theory was they were in fact a cross between cat and rabbit which bred out on the Calf of Man, those 600 acres of detached land at the extreme south, below Spanish Head: now a nature preserve.

Was this any more true than the supposed 'fact' that manx hens lacked tail feathers?

I found myself far more interested in the folk legends and superstitions of the community than a straight forward account of Maughold, the village where Hall Caine was buried and which, most certainly, I should have to see for myself. The origin of the name was rather charming, though. Maughold was an Irish Saint.

He was fettered and set adrift, landing at this point of the island where a fisherman caught a cod and, on gutting it, discovered the key to the Saint's fetters.

Until then I had not imagined any special contact between the island and the Lancashire coastline had existed, but one of the many books I consulted mentioned that between 1670-1765 adventuresome Liverpudlians went to Douglas in order to organise contraband exchanges. The East and West Indiamen, Liverpool bound, found it profitable to stop off at Man to unload silk, tobacco, tea, lace, linen and muslins. From Douglas they were 'run' across the sea to deserted spots upon the Lancashire and Cumberland beaches. One was all too apt to think smuggling confined to Devon and Cornwall or taking place over the Marshes in donkey panniers around the Rye and Winchelsea areas.

Sir Justin did not fail me, though it took him time to collect what I wanted. Indeed I had progressed as far as sketching out the Hall Caine 'appreciation' and filled further notebooks with miscellaneous material by the date his new letter arrived. It seemed that I had set him 'quite a problem'. Parish registers did not always go as far back as one might wish.

Have you been to Somerset House?

This suggestion made me feel guilty for of course I could have done just that. However Sir Justin did produce several fresh facts. Charlotte Goodheart (née Cushing) had lived out her married life at Meadow End farm, a mile or two outside Levens.

Unfortunately it was pulled down to make way for road-widening and I have so far been unable to find anyone who remembers either the house or the tenants thereof.

Charlotte produced three sons, two of whom had emigrated to distant corners of the Commonwealth. Only the eldest had remained to run the farm with his father. There were also girl-twins.

the one called Lavinia, after her aunt, died in infancy. I have been entirely unsuccessful in finding what became of the second girl. Nothing is recorded save the date of their births in 1875 and Lavinia-the-second's death the following year.

This made it sure that Charlotte had married and was well on the way with her family by the year in which her sister of the portrait was killed. The indications were that 'Lavinia two' would have been buried in Ulverston or its vicinity. This he had not had time to verify but the local parson shared the opinion.

There is doubtless a Goodheart family grave. Husband and wife usually are buried together. The child would be with them or very close.

Sir Justin made a vague promise to verify further when he had time but retired though he might be, his local commitments were many and I had no right to expect more from him at this juncture. But for his own admitted interest in the Cushings I might have been granted considerably less.

No doubt it would be fanciful to equate this as further evidence of a dark fate running through certain families. Heaven knows the infant mortality rates were high in the previous century. The child could have died of many diseases prevalent at the time. Croup, typhus, malnutrition—though the latter seemed unlikely in a farming family.

Of course it was tantalising not to know so much as the names of Lavinia Two's three brothers—stalwart lads for sure! Or her twin. But wait! I had read too quickly. The other girl was apparently called Arabella. Arabella Goodheart. Well, it did not sound bad and if, as seemed likely, she survived into young womanhood, doubtless she changed it for that of some man.

It became necessary for me to adopt firm discipline and forget the fascinations of the Cushing Puzzle, since that sixth novel of mine threatened to fall behind schedule if I did not make an effort at completion. Any author will know that there is nothing professionally harder than continuing with something from which any initial sense of glory had long since departed. Of course it had been a mistake to go on holiday when the manuscript was half-way through, although the dates had fitted and I had been feeling in need of some bracing North Country air as antidote to London. True I had left a careful synopsis for the rest of *Hollow Trumpet Sounds*—a title which, in my present disenchanted state, sounded pretentious in the extreme. It was going to take all the professional experience I could muster to dispose of those final chapters. Oh, how little I still cared about characters—so fascinating in the early stages of the book. A wicked, iconoclastic voice inside me was droning *'Kill, kill, kill!'* Send them hurtling from the sky in a burning plane, crashing into the central lane of the M. 1 or perishing in the frothy seas as their ship went down with all hands.

This was the one thing one could *not* do. That charming young lady at my fiction publishers would raise her beautifully shaped eyebrows, pout her pretty mouth and say, 'Really, Mr. Wickham, I don't think we can have that!'

No! I must plod on with them, lacking heart and hope that my general know-how would be sufficient to hide this fact.

When I handed the last batch to Mrs. T for typing she made only one pertinent comment: that my draft seemed to have more alterations than usual.

'I've always said that few literary gentlemen,'—the phrase had long amused me,—'turn in as clear a script as Mr. Wickham.'

'I'm sorry about this one.' It seemed only fair to explain the
40

attendant difficulties. The having gone-away and lost the thread of the story. The lack of interest I did not reveal, because I wished to test her reactions when she had done the typing. Mrs. T struck me as quite a sound model for 'Mrs. Average Reader'.

She did the work expediently: well trained to regard publishers as people continually breathing down the neck of their authors, urging them to 'Hurry! Hurry!'

She heard me come in after a session in the British Museum Reading Room, checking up on a few more Isle of Man essential facts.

'Mr. Wickham! Your book is ready!'

'Splendid! I'll be with you in a jiff!' and I bounded upstairs, singing with relief, having picked up my share of the household post: none of it very interesting. It could wait. My despatch case was dumped on the table by the window, always tidied by Mrs. T, sometimes to my private annoyance.

She had two glasses, a bottle of Empire Sherry and wine biscuits waiting. This was as much a ritual as the pot of tea welcoming guests home after vacations. Despite my mother's misgivings about my conditions in London the life was really very civilised and Mrs. T an exceedingly kind person. Over drinks I asked—casually as I could—what she had thought about the book. (My rather tall frame was deposited not altogether comfortably in a seat a little too low for my length of leg.)

'Do you want my honest opinion, Mr. Wickham?'

'Of course!'

'I liked your other books better.'

I lowered my glass and nodded. That, alas, had become my view as well as hers.

'Any particular reason?'

'Well, it began splendidly,' she admitted. 'The first half was so much better than the second, you know.'

'Ah, ha.'

'It was as if there were a sort of break. Oh I know this sounds silly, Mr. Wickham, but the last chapters could have been written by someone else.'

Veritably my 'slip was showing'! It seemed only fair to confide further in Mrs. T who—bless her—understood just how it had happened. Equating the condition to her own life, she said whenever she came back to No. 183 after going on holiday she 'hated the sight of the place'. Had no desire to roll up blinds, open windows and start on the rooms. For the first few days everything was 'a bind'.

'I wonder why I don't move into a smaller place and just do for myself.'

'Well, why don't you?'

She smiled, admitting that she already had the house and all of us were quite an income, taken into conjunction with the typing, besides which she liked company about the place.

'After two or three days I settle perfectly happily into my old routine.' She looked at me a moment, then, 'When you came back this time, Mr. Wickham, your head was so full of that exciting story about Morecambe Bay Sands that I can understand that those people—' indicating the neatly bound copies of the typescript—'seemed a little dull.' (*Hollow Trumpet Sounds* was about a business firm.)

We had finished our chat and the cheque in payment for the work written and thanked for upon which I went upstairs to begin the task of checking over the book, despatched to my publishers within the next couple of days. The usual 'MS received' card reached me and the book went off to one of the firm's readers. It did not come as altogether a surprise to be asked to call in and see them.

At one time London's publishers were mostly congregated in the precincts of the city. The blitz which destroyed Paternoster Row and so many adjoining streets with literary and newspaper associations, had resulted in gradual dispersal so that in the 1960's publishing houses were to be found in Mayfair, the West Central districts and even in Kensington. Mine were in W.8. Quite close to St. Mary Abbots. The young lady with those well-shaped eyebrows passed me on to her superiors. Mr. Dick, one of the newer directors, would see me. The upshot of the interview was that those trumpets made a sound all too hollow. To some extent he echoed Mrs. T's criticisms.

'Our reader's report really is not very encouraging.'

'Which means?' I hoped my voice did not betray anxiety.

Mr. Dick was reassuring. They would publish, of course, but there were 'some alterations' which, when we had discussed them in detail were going to involve a considerable amount of revision. Metaphorically my heart plummetted! However the job would have to be done.

'Sorry about this,' he said and sounded as if he really meant it.

Returning in chastened mood to No. 183 I cleared my table for action, locking away Sir Justin's recent letter about Lavinia Cushing's niece.

4

The immediate task was naturally to make a satisfactory job of the revisions to my novel and this occupied me to the exclusion of all else. When I took it back it was with the feeling that though it might not be good, at least it was a little better. At all events there were no further hitches with regard to its publication.

Certainly I had not planned to go home again so soon but my father was taken suddenly ill with a coronary and Mother thought it advisable that I should come, which of course I did. He had been whipped into a Harrogate Nursing Home and the most we could do was to visit him at permitted times. No active man could expect to enjoy six weeks of absolute quiet but Father made the best of a bad job in the knowledge that the result could have been so much worse: indeed I wondered if he knew how close he had been to his end. However in those early days he was forced to lie immobile, literally not supposed to lift a finger and to talk very little.

Mother found it all a considerable strain. There was so little I could do in the way of alleviating this except, presumably, being with her and providing not only company, when she would otherwise have been alone, but a reason for making meals; on her own she would have missed out on them.

It was difficult for me to settle to any of my work while I was there, though I did keep up my notes about the Isle of Man and continued reading Mr. Hall Caine. Having lived away from home so long I found the sacrifice of personal liberty hard. It seemed unkind to suggest taking myself off to the local so I just did not go. My parents had their way of life, just as I had mine. What had been a pleasant change on holiday threatened to become very different during an enforced stay of a longer period. Mother was troubled about the expense of it all because they had not joined B.U.P.A. as I once had suggested they should. Night and day nursing at the start would run into a good deal and three weeks was the earliest the doctor would consider Father's return home.

The obvious duty was to offer my financial help which Mother was a little shy of accepting.

'We'll manage, Jake.'

I had to insist. In the end she gave way, even admitting to relief. Probably in common with most people she had a slightly halcyon idea of what authors actually earned from their books. I would not have dreamed of disillusioning her. There were always the G.C.E. scripts, if I ran myself short!

Father was allowed home after his third week, a private nurse in tow for a further few days, after which Mother and the district nurse should manage. His private nurse—whom he was careful to inform us would expect to 'live as family and be addressed as Sister,' was an Australian. Youngish, out-of-doors type, very clear-eyed and forthright—'bossy' was what Mother called it. Sister was instantly interested in me, as an author, having herself known Neville Shute. If there is one thing I abhor it is being quizzed about my profession and she asked all those old, naïve questions. Did I wait for inspiration? Did my books go into lots of editions? Reminding myself that she was in some ways our guest and must therefore be treated with courtesy, I disclaimed any success similar to that of the late Mr. Shute and said, rather facetiously, that the best 'inspiration' any author could have was to see a low bank balance and realise the need to start upon his next book.

Mother lent my first novel to Sister and I wondered what, if anything, she would make of it! She finished it the day before she was due to leave us. Mother was seeing to the evening meal and Sister had settled Father down for a rest before he had his tray of supper.

'You're not awfully good at the love interest, are you, Mr. Wickham?' Placing my book upon the table, jacket-side up.

This was almost as frightful as questioning a man's virility. 'Oh?' I am sure my voice was terse.

'It struck me as being awfully at second-hand, if you know what I mean.'

I did, but had no intention of revealing the fact.

'Take your heroine, Jacey. She doesn't react the way a woman would. And all that "Shall I, shan't I" business! Isn't that pretty old-fashioned?'

'In *Australia*, possibly.'

'In *England*, too, Mr. Wickham. I've been here a couple of years.'

'What would your recipe be, then?' From arrogance my mood was changing to a mild amusement.

'Jump out of the window of your ivory tower, Mr. Wickham.'

'My dear young woman I don't live in one to begin with! I have a bed-sit in London. I'm only up here while my Father—'

She smiled with aggravating calm and reiterated what she had said earlier: that I did not know how to draw a convincing female character in love. We eyed each other from across the

45

table. Was she perhaps expecting me to make a pass at her? If so, she was disappointed.

'I'm not trying to write light romance,' I said coldly.

'I doubt if you'd be much success at it.'

Just then Father's bedside bell tinkled and she went about her professional duties. I wandered aft to the kitchen to see if Mother needed a hand.

'I'm sure that Sister has fallen for your charms, Jake,' stirring something delightful-smelling in a pot.

'Well I haven't for hers!'

'She's quite a nice girl, dear.'

'Maybe.'

'And she's been very good looking after Father.'

'It's her job, isn't it?'

'What's biting you, Jake? I've never known you so restless and moody before. If it's just that you're bored being home, I can manage, now he's over the immediate danger.'

Feeling a double-dyed churl I took my little mother into my arms and said being at home was lovely but I expected we were all suffering from reaction. I can only hope that I was believed...

Sister left. We shook hands politely and never had an occasion to meet again. (I sometimes wonder if she could bring herself to read any more of my books?) Father's condition improved so much that he was raring to be out of bed and dressed but Mother was indomitable in carrying out doctor's wishes.

'You'll want to be off again soon I expect, Jake,' he said, when I was sitting in his room with him.

'No hurry.'

'Thought my number was up this time. Afraid your mother must have had a bad scare.'

'We both did.'

'Jake. Take care of her if I do anything silly like this again, won't you?'

My promise was readily given.

'We both realise you have your own life to live down in London. But—don't leave it too long before you look us up next time, will you?'

'No.' In fact I told him that I should have to go to the Isle of Man shortly and would stop off *en route* for Liverpool. This pleased him and presently his head began to nod. It was terrible how quickly he grew tired, though I assumed this phase would pass.

The news of Father's illness had reached Sir Justin, who very kindly phoned through to enquire progress and seemed pleased that I should be the one to answer.

'Suppose you wouldn't like to spend the night on your way back?' The tone was provocative. Had he perhaps some fresh information lined-up for me about the Cushing family and its descendants?

'I should love to, Sir Justin.'

'Any idea when you'll be leaving?'

I told him and he arranged to meet me at Grange.

My parents were sorry to see me go and, in a way, I to leave them. Father would have to take care for the next few months but there was no reason to regard himself as a permanent invalid. Mother was brave over my departure when I knew she would have liked me to remain on but she accepted that I had commitments, as was true.

It was pleasant to find myself once more in Grange-over-Sands and to recognise Sir Justin's car waiting for me. He asked for the latest bulletin upon Father, saying at the end of this:

'Then he isn't in danger any longer?'

'Apparently not, so long as he exercises care: very little in the way of drink and cutting down on smoking.'

Talk turned to other matters on the two mile drive into Cartmel. At the house 'Kate' Hardcastle welcomed me, saying that they were delighted to have me with them again and had given me my old room.

Downstairs the portrait of Lavinia Cushing drew me towards it even more compellingly. There was nothing of the peasant about her figure. The sheen of the silk of her dress still struck me as being a masterpiece of the painter's art. The poise of the head was exquisite. I could almost imagine her advancing to meet me, eyes full of enquiry, the tilt of the chin so proud.

'Ah! Still mooning around Lavinia, Wickham? I can see you making me an offer for her one of these days.'

'You wouldn't sell?'

'With what could I replace such a portrait? Let us say she is the magnet to draw you back to Cartmel. Shall we have a sherry before dinner?' He went to the door and called. 'Kate! Sherrytime.'

From the muffled precincts of somewhere in the house we heard her reply of 'Coming, dear.'

Over dinner she said that my enquiries had provided her husband with a brand new interest.

'A revived one, my dear,' he pointed out. 'I was always intrigued by the Cushing legend.'

'And have you something fresh for me?'

He mentioned a very old man living over at Lindale just outside Grange. Rising ninety and eccentric as they came, the ancient nevertheless had a phenomenal memory for things past although events of a recent nature were forgotten. The Hardcastles did charitable work of one kind and another around the district.

'Old people like one to drop in for a chat. Loneliness is probably their greatest single ailment, Wickham. Some go into homes—good or bad—others end their days in a geriatric ward. A few stay put, dependent upon other people only in so far as they have to be. This old fellow Dan is half blind and doesn't hear as well as he did but he is remarkably active. Used to be a shepherd. Hard life, no doubt, yet healthy. There isn't much local history that he doesn't know. So I thought we might try him. Don't know why I didn't think of it before—'

'When can we go? Really I ought to return to town tomorrow—' hesitating, then—'well, at any rate on the next day.'

In the morning which was wonderful and fine we took a couple of sticks and walked to Lindale, Sir Justin giving me some last minute tips as to how to deal with the shepherd.

'Daniel Priddy's the name.'

We carried with us some dainties made up into a parcel which Sir Justin carried in a khaki respirator case from the last war. The cottage where Priddy lived was a minute but-and-ben nicely set near the dales he must have walked so often in the course of his long outdoor life. He had a grand-daughter, coming up towards middle-age, living a few doors away and according to Sir Justin she did little enough for the old man. Extenuating circumstances by way of husband and children might be made out for the woman, Sir Justin supposed.

'Take a deep breath before you enter, Wickham, old Daniel's home doesn't smell exactly sweet!'

The minute cottage windows were tight shut. It was doubtful whether they had been opened for years. The front door was ajar, revealing a flight of precipitous stairs to the upper floor. Sir Justin knocked on an inner door to our right and a querulous voice asked who it was. Sir Justin enunciated clearly and was given grudging permission to enter.

In a chair well away from draughts sat an old, old man, a plaid across bony knees and carpet-slippered feet peeping out of it. He made as if to stand up but Sir Justin signalled otherwise as he introduced me. The fact that I wrote books did not impress. The table had one of those chenille cloths with pompoms. On it were the remains of his own breakfast plus a cup, saucer and plate (dusty but unused) placed before an empty chair drawn up to table. On the back of the chair was a woman's coat so old that it was dropping to pieces.

'Wife's,' said Priddy, evidently a laconic character.

Though Sir Justin had warned me in advance the effect of that coat on the empty chair back was macabre and put me in mind of *Great Expectations*. Perhaps Dickens' 'Miss Havisham' of Satis House sitting around in her ancient wedding dress with the cobwebbed cake uncut was not after all a bizarre figure of imagination but someone he actually had met. A kind of Dan Priddy in fact.

We had to partake of the grand-daughter's cowslip wine which was good, though I felt doubtful about the glasses. However they say we swallow a peck of dirt in our lifetime!.

There had to be a good deal of explaining and prompting before Daniel could be persuaded to talk about what we wanted to hear. His memory did not of course go as far back actually as Lavinia Cushing, though he knew vaguely of the fishing tragedy by now doubtless a local legend. His father, who had lived to a good age himself, we gathered, had heard tell of the Davage shooting. Nothing fresh here.

'Recollect the Goodhearts though.'

Dan described where their farm Meadow End had been and what John Goodheart himself was like: shrewd, close, a drinker on Fair Days but on the whole well liked. Priddy senior had been his cowman. Charlotte, who must have been middle-aged in the late 1880's to 90's when Dan might be said to have been a young man, was described as 'the sad lady'.

'What did she look like, Mr. Priddy? Can you remember at all?'

If he did, he lacked words to describe her. I had to be content with a vague shape sketched by his gnarled hands, greying hair, rosy complexion and blue eyes—at least he *thought* they had been blue. She had worked hard on the farm, making huge meals for the men as they came off the fields to eat at the large kitchen table. Rising early to help milk, churning butter and baking bread, not to mention the curing of hams and preserve-making activities of those days. Priddy knew that two sons had gone abroad (their names are not important), whilst the eldest, Ben, had—as we already knew—remained behind to run Meadow End.

'Never married. Not he.'

Ben had inherited the family bad luck to the extent of being gored by a bull from which accident he never recovered.

'Had to be shot.'

One hoped that Dan had meant the bull and not the wretched Ben!

'What became of the farm?' I put the question carefully.

'Sold 'un.'

Charlotte and John Goodheart would have been dead by then, if my memory of the date given me by Sir Justin was correct.

'You wouldn't be able to tell us anything about the girl?'

'Died as a we'un.'

'Not Lavinia. The one who lived. Arabella.'

'Her?' He shook his crop of snowy curls. 'Went away.'

By this time Dan was looking exhausted and we made a move, gulping in great gusts of fresh air directly we emerged into the welcoming open.

'Hope that satisfied you, Wickham,' said Sir Justin, as we set off again determined to follow up the cowslip wine with some local beer and a sandwich or two.

'It certainly gives me some interesting sidelines on the descendants of the Cushings, but all the same I'd like to know what became of Arabella.'

At that juncture I had no idea that I should discover that—and more—in the most unexpected circumstances!

PART 2

ARABELLA GOODHEART

Since Thomas Henry Hall Caine was not, in fact, a full Manxman—his mother was from Cumberland—I would need to take a look at Runcorn where he actually had been born in 1863. Also it seemed advisable to present something of his earlier careers as architect and journalist. (Back files of journals and periodicals were apt to have been affected by blitz losses.) However I did what I could between the *Liverpool Mercury* and *The Athenaeum*. Caine's recollections of Rossetti and three centuries of sonnets (both 1882) and critical cobwebs of the following year were not to be totally ignored in favour of his better-known novels, some of which had been dramatised: 'Caine in the Theatre', a later chapter! Nor could I ignore his important work in promoting the International Copyright Movement. Quite a traveller, too, before he settled at Greeba Castle, Isle of Man, which judging by the pictures, was a fastness in a delightful setting.

It seemed a pity to waste the flying time to Ronaldsway airport so I settled down with *The Shadow of a Crime*, having reached the trial of 'Ralph Ray' in Carlisle.

I had just reached the passage following the reprieve where a mighty shout went up:

It was one vast voice, more loud than the blast on the mountains, more deep than the roar of the sea!

When in a very much smaller and more modern voice, the hostess was telling us to fasten our safety belts as we were about to touch down upon Manx territory.

The 13 year old airport struck me as pleasantly sited and a hired car took me 'down' to Douglas, 'up', so I was informed, being used only for Castletown, the former capital. It was not necessarily my intention to stay in Douglas for more than a night or so: it merely seemed the obvious initial choice.

Douglas proved to be most of what I had been led to expect, a modern, well laid out resort with quaintly archaic horse drawn trams and the electric railway running to Laxey and Ramsey, Snaefell branch line being a 2034 ascent.

Victoria Pier where the steamers docked was 1872 vintage and, lying offshore, a Tower of Refuge—designed by Hansom of the cabs fame—marked the dangerous Conister Rocks.

Before bed I took a look at the Marina Gardens and did a dutiful perambulation along the Central Promenade of this land where 'Nobody is somebody' as the Manx proverb had it: a statement in direct contradiction of W.S. Gilbert's theory (expressed in *The Gondoliers*) that once everybody became somebody, nobody was anybody!

Since rain greeted me next morning there seemed no better pre-lunch plan than a visit to the National Museum, a somewhat displeasing shade of red brick on the outside but inside, quite the best of its kind it had ever been my fortune to come across. Not only were the exhibits excellently displayed but they were legibly written-up and well-lit. The Manx names of Christian, Kermode, Quail, Quinn and Qualtrough seemed prevalent. The folk section in particular fascinated me and I resolved to spend longer there on some future occasion.

Next day I hired a car and did a prospecting tour of some of the better known glens, diverting to take in the Spooyt Vane (white spout) waterfall, better than Becky Fall in Devon, the pre-historic burial ground (circle of Mull) and so back across the Roundtable mountain spine of the island. From Douglas I moved on to Peel, 'the sunset city' immortalised by Scott's story of Peel Tower from which 'Fenella' made her sensational leap after her lover 'Julian Peverel'. (Until that morning the name Peverel had been fixed in my mind as being of the peak district.) Anyway they had named one of the island trains after Fenella.

56

The corner of Peel harbour—for some reason—was known as the Kremlin.

No one could be there and ignore the thriving herring curing industry.

'We produce about six million a year,' they told me where I went to order some pairs for my parents as well as the Hardcastles and the inestimable Mrs. T. Manx kippers had been on the breakfast menu that very morning so there was no question of taking their reputation on hearsay. Nor was there any difficulty about seeing over the Curtis herring factory, where machines gutted and cleaned; vats of brine salted the fish before they were hung upon wooden poles above special oak-chip fires.

'Each one stays for 15-20 hours before it can be called a kipper, sir.'

How far these activities enhanced the background of Hall Caine's writing would be hard to say. Nor, I feel, could one justifiably include as vital that visit to the lighthouse at Point of Ayre to indulge a boyhood delight in such places. The vista at the top of those endlessly curving stairs was indeed worth the climb. Ireland in front of me, Scotland over my right shoulder and, behind me, Cumberland! Even the American who had been one of our party conceded it to be 'Quite a view.'

Legitimate surely, my visit to the 'show' village of Creigneish which perpetuated the old crafts inside a series of cottages topped by thatching in a style peculiar to the island. The straw roofs were crossed at intervals of from 12-18 inches by ropes of thatch, secured to the walls by projecting stones. It seemed obvious the idea was practical as well as ornamental, securing the roof against the worst winds that blew across from Bradda Head. One of the cottages belonged to Mr. Harry Kelly.

'The original "Kelly from the Isle of Man"?' I quipped.

He laughed, shaking his head and explaining that there had been a great number of Irish and Scots settlers.

'Will you have been to Niarbyl Cove yet, sir? There's Florrie

Ford's cottage down on the beach. She was the lady who used to sing about your Kelly.'

That a music hall artist's house should have been evolved into a tourist attraction seemed a little strange.

'I suppose you're well up in all the local legends and folk lore, Mr. Kelly?'

From him I heard of the two celebrated ghosts: 'the grey lady of Castletown' and 'Moddey Dhoo' the black dog of Peel Castle whose appearance presaged death. Even if my obliging informant was unable to give actual instances one might argue that it depended upon how much—or how little—one was prepared to believe.

'I trust you always remember to greet the little people each time you cross the white Fairies Bridge on the way to Douglas, sir?'

'I was told *that* as soon as I arrived and I duly say "Good morning" or "Good night Little People" as the case may be.'

'Should take off the hat to them too, sir.' He eyed my bare head with amusement before adding that few people wore hats these days. 'You'll have heard the origin of the Isle of Man?'

He recounted the legend of how two giants—resident in Ireland and Cumberland respectively—loved the same girl and fought for her. Victory went to Ireland. As the defeated Cumbrian giant retreated to his native hills, the Irish one grabbed a handful of earth and flung it after him. It fell short, landing halfway between the two countries. And to prove the genuineness of the story one only had to compare the shape of Mona with Lough Neagh over in Ireland: the 'hole' which the missing clod formed!

Mr. Kelly shook his head sadly, saying that it was always unfortunate when two men loved the same woman.

My prospective publishers of the Hall Caine book had given me a letter of introduction to an author of theirs living in Ramsey, thinking that it might interest us to meet. I knew

58

nothing about Miss Blanche Quinn M.A. except that she was a Manxwoman and presumably somewhat of an authority on matters relating to the island. So I telephoned and was bidden to lunch, making the trip via Kirk Michael in order to take an outward glance at Bishops Court where the Lord Bishop of the Diocese of Soder and Man had his residence. Theoretically the island was Free Church. Nevertheless it had its own Convocation and officials. The Bishop could issue marriage licences 'at any time or place'.

On into 'Royal' Ramsey, so called because of Queen Victoria's visit, a tower above the town commemorating a view which the Prince Consort graciously admired!

Miss Quinn's house lay well back from the popular sector in one of the leafy residential areas and was called—with singular lack of originality—Mona Villa.

Miss Quinn proved elderly, mildly eccentric as is often the case with scholars, but hospitable in the extreme. She sailed like a galleon, a big woman with carefully arranged, thinning hair and a kind of age-less button-through type of frock. She had most of the Manx characteristics: modesty over her achievements, a degree of Celtic mysticism and fervour, and a wish to live in peace. Moreover she spoke the language which comparatively few of the natives still did.

'A number of the children know the Lord's Prayer in Manx, but that's about all. Oh and the countryfolk may occasionally greet one another in Manx, Mr. Wickham. But you should never joke with us until you've known us at least thirty years!'

Over excellent sherry she ran through some of the place-names which had puzzled me, thus it was that Balla stood for a homestead or farm, cronk or knock meant hill, and slieu, mountain.

'You can trace the Scandinavian in such words as "by" farm, Colby, for instance. Vick, meaning a small creek, is also Scandinavian. Manx Gaelic is closest to the Scotch and Irish variety.'

I learned, too, how the race waters at the end of Point of Ayre bore the local name of 'strews' and the Manx for wells was *chibbyrs*.

'Many are mere grottos but several are supposed to have fertility powers. You should, perhaps, make a note of the one at Maughold Head in what we might call the Caine country. You've seen his memorial in the churchyard over there? So massive! A sort of Trajan's Column, only in grey! However! As I was about to tell you, Mr. Wickham, some of the well water is said to alleviate the pangs of childbirth but, as you'll appreciate, I cannot speak from any *personal* knowledge!'

She expressed surprise that any publisher should be bothering about Hall Caine in the 1960's

'Let's face it, by modern standards his style is considerably larger than life. My father left me a complete set of Hall Caine's works and I trust you'll feel free to borrow any you may need.'

I had a sense that she was poking mild fun at the project as she took me into her library, a huge room with ceiling to wall shelving.

'There, Mr. Wickham—' indicating volume after volume of leather-bound Hall Caine. Regrettably, perhaps, I was more interested in such island 'histories' as the Stenning one. She slipped out a slim book, written by herself, (on the Manx language,) of which I was delighted to have the loan. There were a number of water colour views—none exactly remarkable, but all of them pleasant in their pastel styles: Port Erin, Castle Rushen, Arbory on Fair Day, and the monk's bridge at Ballasalla: 'oldest in the island' according to Miss Quinn.

The library tour was interrupted for a lunch, excellent as the sherry which had preceded it.

After our meal she entertained me with a variety of stories about the Island. Did I know, for example, that there was still a law making it permissible to shoot any Scot on sight because Robert the Bruce had been a particularly unjust ruler of the islands and expelled all Scots?

'You'll have noticed they've come back, despite the threat to their. lives!'

Amongst the old statutes was one known as 'Rope, Sword or Ring'. In effect it gave any girl 'taken without consent' (a euphemism, presumably, for rape or something pretty near it) and bearing a child, the choice to subject a man responsible to one of three things:

'A rope with which to be hanged. A sword for decapitation, or a ring to marry. the girl.'

'And are there any instances of this ever having taken place, Miss Quinn?'

'Indeed yes. I have some notes about it amongst the papers I am collecting for a book on our legends. There have been others, but I rather hope that mine may prove the more complete.' She rummaged around in one of those small Victorian desks always associated in my mind with the Brönte sisters. 'Here we are.' And she handed me an account of how one Roger Kermode, of the Manx Fencibles (the regiment sent to stem the Irish Rebellion in 1798) had raped a maid-servant. out at Trammon Tree Farm in the Andreas region.

'If you're thinking this Roger may be related to the many respectable Kermodes, Mr. Wickham, I must remind you that on this island, as on most others, a great deal of inter-marriage takes place. In fact we have a saying that if a person has the same name as ours he's no relation but if he happens to have a *different* name, then he's probably a cousin.'

I was not really attending to what she had been saying, being anxious to reach the end of the quaint story. The rascally Roger had been duly brought to justice and the girl unhesitatingly selected the rope for which in the circumstances one could not, perhaps, entirely blame her. No sooner was her 'despoiler strung up' than she relented in favour of the ring.

' "The accused was forthwith cut down and being offered the ring, refused to accept it, saying that a man could not be punished twice for the same crime." '

One imagined the reprieved Roger rubbing his neck—wincing slightly no doubt as he did so—then clicking his heels, bowing and marching up the road out of sight.

'The story had a relatively happy ending,' Miss Quinn was saying, 'In as much as the farmer married the girl and brought up the child as if it were his own.'

We smiled over the amusing anecdote from the past. She believed that Roger's branch of the Kermode family were still around.

'In fact a descendant of his married a Lancashire girl called —as I recollect it—Arabella Goodheart.'

'Arabella Goodheart, did you say? And could she possibly have come from Levens, near Kendal?'

Miss Quinn looked surprised by my sudden excitement. Did I then know something about Arabella?

'Possibly. One of the grand-daughters of a fishing family called Cushing bore that name,' and briefly I sketched in the genealogical details. My listener looked extremely interested, questioning me exhaustively before saying with an impressive finality:

'I believe this Arabella of yours, Mr. Wickham, must indeed be one and the same person.'

'And is there anything you can tell me about her?' My pre-occupation with the Cushings and those connected with them was just about understandable, though Miss Quinn would be bound to mistake it for a purely academic interest when in fact it was so much more.

'Tell you about Arabella Goodheart, you mean? Oh yes! In fact she played a part in another of our Manx stories. Rather a sad one, I'm afraid.'

Could one expect it to have been otherwise, for a niece of Lavinia Cushing?

Almost a century separated the lives of Roger Kermode and Arabella Goodheart. There had to be a link. The intervening material was sketchy to say the least and it was not pieced together by me in one single visit to Miss Quinn: nor indeed was she my only source of information. However she was kind enough to invite me to her house on a second and even a third occasion. And at each visit she had something fresh either to show or to recount....

In brief then, Roger—finding the island uncongenial, perhaps, after his experiences—went to the mainland to settle. So far as was known—in Liverpool, where he married and had a son, Jocelyn, who went to sea. Miss Quinn had an idea that the young man had been one of the 52 persons rescued from the *Parkfield* in 1833.

The dangers to shipping in Douglas Bay do not have to be stressed. The story, as she told it, was that both the lifeboats from the first Douglas station (established originally in 1802) were sent out to assist.

'Douglas was one of the earliest places in the British Isles to be provided with a lifeboat, Mr. Wickham, we're justly proud of this fact.'

'I thought I understood you to say *two* lifeboats stood by on this *Parkfield* vessel?'

'So they did.'

Douglas's first lifeboat was sent them in 1802 being one of 31 by Henry Greathead, builder of the first lifeboat stationed at the mouth of the Tyne (1789). A second was requested in 1824 'on account of the frequent gales and wrecks in Douglas Bay' and arrived in October 1825. Two years later a larger ten-oared boat came into service, remaining in use until 1851.

'The boats appear to have worked in conjunction at this

period,' and Miss Quinn had taken the trouble on my behalf to check with the Ramsey lifeboat coxswain.

Between 1824 and 1851, ninety-one lives were saved.

'Coxswain Isaac Vandy was voted two silver medals, I'm told, for his part in the *Parkfield* rescue operation.'

From that time onward Roger Kermode continued to be ever more elusive. Miss Quinn thought it safe to conclude that he remained at sea and was believed to have died abroad: around the 1870's.

'Of typhoid, black fever or some such,' she hazarded.

'Did he marry?'

'Oh, yes, a Manx girl. A Heywood. Distant connection of Middy Heywood of the Bounty Mutiny. You'll have seen Hague Farmhouse on Summerhill Road where Captain Bligh spent his honeymoon? She, too, was a local and it's interesting to note that Christian and the Heywood boy likewise were Manxmen. Incidentally, there's a well in the farmyard.'

I could not quite see the point of her mentioning this though a twinkle and a smile suggested more was to come.

'As I mentioned once before, I think Manx wells often have very special properties, Mr. Wickham. I'm not sure whether this particular one did, or not. Over at Port Erin now, near the station, you'll find St. Catherine's well. There an aging woman might drink and become as a girl of seventeen again! However I fancy the water in St. Catherine's drained away long ago.'

Miss Heywood (or Mrs. Jocelyn Kermode as she should be called) produced stalwart, sea-loving sons who confined themselves to the local herring fishing (there were few fresh water varieties on the island).

'On what part of Man did these lads live, Miss Quinn?'

'Port St. Mary.'

'Ah! The place where the lifeboat is always at anchor in the harbour. I've often wondered why that is.'

She did not know for sure but suggested a slipway accident in 1937 at a launching practice might be the reason. Apparently

64

the four men working the winch were thrown from the handles, one of the men receiving fatal injuries.

'Manx fisherfolk are very superstitious, Mr. Wickham. For instance if the sun doesn't shine over Peel Hill on New Year's Day, it'll be a bad day for herring fishing. The men also hold the firm belief that the third boat to leave harbour when the fleet puts out will have no luck. For that reason the second and third boats are lashed together.'

We agreed that this seemed cheating the fates, as it were.

'You wouldn't know the origin for this odd belief, Miss Quinn?'

She said that no one was certain but the consensus of opinion, was that it had to do with the idea of the Trinity and no one 'wishing to become the Holy Ghost.' She went on speaking:

'This third idea persists in another form, too. That of the third day. The spirit is supposed to haunt the body for two days after death so to hold a funeral *before* the third day would be to—er—limit the spirit's chances in afterlife.'

'What an extraordinary thought!'

'Logical though if you accept the premise in the first place.' (I was not at all sure that I did.)

'Fishermen are also very keen to procure a Bollan'—a Manx charm: a seafish with a triangular set of teeth in the gullet. 'Men give them to their sweethearts to ensure fidelity or just throw them into the air to indicate the direction for a good catch of fish. Most prized possession of the lot, of course,' added Miss Quinn, 'is a caul.'

'Isn't that to ensure against drowning?'

There was a tale—she did not attempt to vouch for the truth of it—that Jocelyn Kermode had been born with a caul over his head which accounted for the fact that he was saved from the *Parkfield*.

'And did the fifty-one other survivors also have cauls?' I asked, smiling a little.

And so to Port St. Mary itself, a charmingly quiet and rather

Cornish looking place with celebrated chasms and a plateau of black-grey rocks not unlike pictures I had seen of the Giant's Causeway, though upon a smaller scale. The cliff walk to Spanish Head, so named because of an Armada galleon was wrecked off it, I had already enjoyed. Now my first objective was the quay with the thriving winter seasonal fishing for and processing of scollops—a lucrative island export. Nothing much was happening. Only a few small craft rode at anchor under the benign chaperonage of *The R.A. Colby Cubbin No. 2*, as the lifeboat was called.

Quite obviously the Town Hall was what I required. In a grimly utilitarian room formidable looking Manx officials stared coldly down from fading photographs, mustering between them as fine a display of whiskerage as it had been my privilege to see. Again those reoccurring local names: Qualtrough, Kneen and, of course, Kermode. Which—if any—of these severely correct gentlemen might have been those fishermen sons of Jocelyn?

It would be deluding myself to pretend that any of these enquiries had the slightest bearing upon the Hall Caine book, but ever since I had seen that portrait of Lavinia Cushing at Cartmel I knew I should never be really satisfied until I had found out all that I could about her descendants. And knowing that her own niece, Arabella Goodheart, was somehow connected with the Isle of Man, how could I give up the researchs half way through completion?

Of course it all took time!

When I reported back to my good friend Miss Quinn upon the third occasion, it had been established that the Kermode-Heywood alliance yielded four sons, one of whom had followed an old island precedent of emigrating to the United States. (Two of Charlotte Goodheart's sons had emigrated in their day, leaving but one behind in England.) As I already knew, two Kermodes became Port St. Mary fishermen whilst the fourth and remaining youth drifted across the mainland. There is no record of his returning to the island and in any case he was not the link with Arabella. Miss Quinn took up this section of the story.

'Arabella came over about the turn of the century, when she'd have been twenty-five or thereabouts. It may have been on holiday or to take up work. Since only the well-to-do had vacations in those days, a job is the more likely explanation.'

Every Sixth of August since 1897 when the flag pole was first supplied to the Port St. Mary lifeboat station, an exercise was held, preceded by the firing of the maroon by the coxswain. The launching of any lifeboat whether for exercise or duty call always carried with it local excitement. People rushed to the quay to watch and to shout 'She's away!' Among them will have been Arabella Goodheart.

I had seen photographs of those two Kermode brothers and while there cannot be said to be any specific Manx type—as there are of Cornish and Welshmen—a certain dash seems inherent in the wearers of navy sweaters, serge trousers and thigh-level wading boots. And Arabella's grandfather Cushing had been a fisherman. There was bound to have seemed a natural affinity with those who put out to sea with the herring fleets, and loss of which has been commemorated in one of the Manx folk songs. And they say these men will pick the *clagh bane* (whitestone) out of the very ballast they use.

'Lest it cause disaster,' pointed out Miss Quinn, making me *au fait* with yet another of the strange superstitions of the islanders. 'It probably dates back to the Neolithic graves being of whitestone.'

But to return to these Port St. Mary brothers. Jarlath Kermode (an Irish element emerging here) was the elder: a fine, upstanding, laughing man, broad-chested and immensely strong, but not above middle height. His brother Gabriel was known as *'cabbyl-ushteg'* by his friends being thought to resemble the Manx merman or, as some unkindly call it, waterbull, given to inviting people to ride on his back before disappearing with them into the sea. The Europa legend again.

Jarlath fell in love with Arabella and from the photograph

67

one would have thought him the more attractive of the two, but it was to the redhead Gabriel she gave her heart.

'He was not a very nice man, Mr. Wickham. Brave I daresay, but a bit of a ram, if you understand me.'

Gabriel had a way with a woman and he married Arabella at harvest time 1902 (according to the parish register), a period of parish teas and in the olden days, of the *Mhellia* or corn dolly in every farm. The young couple lived in one of the fishermen's cottages near the quay and whatever the jealousy that may have existed between the two brothers, their very livelihood kept their working lives in a closeness from which there could be little escape. Their boat, the *Glashtyn* (a kind of waterhorse) continued to go out with the nets.

The year drew to its close.

'New Year's Day is a great occasion in the island, more important really than Christmas itself. A disastrous year lies ahead if a cat crosses the threshold so steps are taken to see that all cats are kept in on the eve. The first footer or *Qualtugh* as we call him, must be dark for preference. A red head is virtually useless: a woman worse even than a cat.'

Arabella had a pet cat, just an ordinary long-tailed tabby to which she was devoted and being a queen with an eye for some bitten-eared tom no doubt, slipped out and stayed out on New Year's Eve.

'Of course there is no reason to imagine that this had a thing to do with what followed,' Miss Quinn conceded, though it featured in the account of subsequent events.

Gabriel had gone out looking for the cat, to please his wife who was by that time pregnant and he met up with convivial companions who persuaded him to celebrate.

Jarlath, who had been 'booked' for first foot was on his way to the cottage when he passed his brother reeling drunkenly along the quay. Disgusted with Gabriel and mindful of Arabella's condition, Jarlath tried to persuade his brother to sober-up before returning home.

'Mind your own bloody business' Gabriel was reported to have shouted.

Late though the hour was, there were people abroad.

Jarlath made a grab at him, intending to lead his brother quietly but Gabriel slipped and fell into the harbour, hitting his head as he did so. Jarlath dived in, fully clothed, as did one of the other locals; they were strong swimmers all. Gabriel was brought to the surface after repeated diving efforts and hauled up on to the quay, where they enacted artificial respiration unavailingly. At last Jarlath rose, shaking his head. Someone ought to go to Arabella and prepare her for the shock of her husband's death. The only woman present—she had come out at the sound of the splash and the shouts—was a redhead.

'We can imagine that Arabella will have taken the news stoically—in the manner of her kind.'

I could picture the sad procession up from the harbour, Jarlath leading, the covered body of his drowned brother on a stretcher or possibly just a sheet of boat canvas. The slow tramp of sodden boots, the pause and then the stopping outside No. 5 fisher's row. Arabella, already large with child, waiting beside her red-headed neighbour. Then the silent progress up incredibly steep and awkward stairs before the laying of him down upon the brass bedstead the couple would have shared.

Miss Quinn described for me a Manx Funeral.

'The coffin is brought outside the house or cottage and placed upon two chairs. Friends collect and stand reverently around it, the Vicar with them. Suitable hymns—the old "bardoons" very often—are sung.'

The coffin is then placed upon a bier or hearse: horse-drawn doubtless in the case of Gabriel Kermode. The relatives and friends follow slowly on foot.

'According to tradition no new road must be taken by the coffin which, as you'll appreciate, may call for a certain ingenuity of route on some occasions. It is customary for relatives to remain seated throughout the service and to attend—

still in mourning—the following Sunday, when they do the same.'

There is little more that has to be said regarding Arabella, who was fortunate to carry her child to full-term and in 1903 gave birth to a daughter, Gabrielle Kermode.

3

It must not be assumed that all work upon Hall Caine had ceased in order to indulge a purely private interest. Nor, should it be thought that I was not, in fact, turning over ideas for the next novel. This process was leisurely in my case but once a theme had been found, the plot to illustrate it took less long to prepare and the actual writing-up, comparatively few months.

At Miss Quinn's suggestion I had moved into Ramsey which allowed me to be nearer her and to enjoy pleasant after coffee visits to Mona Villa. Our friendship, though largely of an academic kind, was nevertheless rewarding for me and prevented the sort of loneliness that could beset an hotel-based bachelor on a strange island. The people one met in the lounge and elsewhere were the richer industrialist types from the Midlands and the North : family parties, many late middle-aged or older. Discussion seemed to centre around prevailing winds— which I admit were often displeasing—and why it was not warmer for the time of year.

'There's a 'fluence on the weather,' remarked a jolly little man who was lonelier far than myself. Through him I came to do the walk along the marine drive coastal road between Douglas and Port Soderic—an excellent example of what can be achieved with rather unpromising beach material, also to join him on the motor boat mail and stores delivery run from

Port St. Mary round the Calf of Man, that strange little island —beyond—an—island. Landing by visitors was not permitted in the nesting season between early May and late July.

The boatman who knew me already nodded his head in greeting as the little party climbed aboard. The boat was more covered in than the ex-lifeboat craft that plied between the various Isles of Scilly.

'They say the Calf is bigger than Monaco,' my 'Fluence friend, Mr. Potts observed, having insisted upon joining me which I did not in the least resent.

'About six hundred acres,' the boatman told us. 'It rises to four hundred and twenty feet at the highest point,' a pipe was gestured in the direction. 'There were two lighthouses in use back in eighteen eighteen but since the Chickens one has been built, the old one is not used.'

'Why "Chickens"?' someone put the question I had been about to ask.

This lighthouse was situated upon a tidal reef some three quarters of a mile to the south of Calf. The name was probably acquired in about 1875 and the boatman's guess, that it had to do with stormy petrels: 'Mother Carey's chickens.'

Our boatman promised us herring gulls, fulmar petrels, also choughs and, with luck, a few grey seals. Herons, he said, were to be found on Langness point, which was in Castletown Bay.

There was a National Trust warden living on the Calf, the buildings of which consisted of one farm and the living accommodation thereof: sizable at that: eleven rooms, each with h & c and they had their own electric generator. Mr. Potts had been across when it was not the closed season and told me that there was a Latin inscription above the door of the farm-house which, translated, meant 'The little House in the Great Peace'.

Here our boatman took up the story, telling us that the National Trust had acquired the land in 1930.

'Used to be a pub over there once,' he murmured remini-scently. There were the remains of Bushels House, which was said to have been erected by a gentleman of that name in Queen Elizabeth I's reign.

'Murdered some lady and fled there from justice.'

There was also supposed to be a Viking's look out, which I could readily accept as they figured so much in early Manx history and a 'mock' invasion carnival was held annually in Peel when the longboats again sailed in to the shore.

'The Calf is just a nature preserve?' I asked, leaning over the side to admire stupendous, frightening rocks with their ledge-dwelling sea birds.

'That's right, sir.'

We were drawing close to Craigher Point when Mr. Potts informed everyone mail and provisions would be delivered. Quay proper there was none. The boat nosed carefully into a natural haven barely wide enough to receive us. The engines cut. Our approach was seen and probably heard too in a stillness complete save for the sound of the sea. A young man began scrambling and slithering down the rock towards us. He did not seem very sure of the route and lacked the deeply tanned, outdoor look of the boat and trawlermen. He squatted to remove shoes and socks, his feet and legs looking almost indecently pale: rolled up trousers to the knee then waded into seaweedy water: a tall blond youth of good physique but who seemed more a city dweller than an out-of-doors type.

'Catch!'

Just that single instruction as first the mail, then the carton of provisions went over the side. Almost at once the engine was re-started and we went out astern. The strong smell of shag tobacco was borne towards those of us who were nearest the boatman. Having steered safely clear he turned direction for the homeward run, saying to me casually as you like:

'That young fellow's a connection of the family you were so interested in.'

'The Kermodes, you mean?'

The boatman drew reflectively on his pipe. No that was not the name, nevertheless he was sure there was a connection.

72

The lad did not live on the island. He had 'come from some college or another as I heard it.'

This was intriguing and, at the same time rather irritating. In fact it took me several days to place Mr. Pale-legs correctly.

When Arabella Kermode's daughter, Gabrielle, was born, Arabella herself not unnaturally had a very bad time of it, strong countrywoman though she was. She lived a quiet life centred upon her baby, entering into nothing that went on in Port St. Mary. After a while well-intentioned neighbours gave up trying to include her. As the story was told me by an old woman who had known Arabella, she went around like a pale ghost, gravely greeting those she met when she carried out her modest shopping. A fund had been collected for her—one gathered at the instigation of Jarlath, whose devotion became deepened by personal recrimination at having been unable to save his brother's life and, who shall say? by a terrible wondering if the fall might not have been prevented. Had some gesture of Jarlath's indirectly led to the death lurch?.

It was not fashionable to say that people died from broken hearts but that was how it appeared to have been with Arabella. Daily she grew thinner, clothes hanging as on a scarecrow. Her bonny country colouring faded. Her cheeks sank in: her eyes lost their lustre.

One could imagine Jarlath's distress. It was said that he would have liked to have married her, thereby providing a life of less want, but I fancy that it was only in more recent years that marriage between brother and sister-in-law became legalised—if, indeed Arabella would have countenanced such a proposition. One suspects not. Even if she did not blame Jarlath for her husband's death at least Jarlath's presence must have been an eternal reminder of that sad New Year's Eve.

Arabella grew more than ever of a shadow. Nothing could rouse her, much less make her smile. Even tending the child was becoming too great an effort in her state of health. Some said she starved herself to death. Others that she pined herself into a premature grave. Whether the cause was either—or

c*

a mixture of both—she died within two years of Gabriel's drowning.

Again all the solemnity of a Manx funeral from fisher's row…

Arabella was buried in St. Mary's churchyard in the same grave as that of her husband.

The baby was cared for by Jarlath who married a worthy body of the town, not because he loved her but because some sort of a mother was needed for his sweetheart's child. By all accounts the marriage, however unromantically begun, turned out to be more than averagely happy but childless they remained. That had not apparently concerned them, since there was little Gabrielle. She grew up happy and carefree, educated at the local school, in and out of the sea with the other children, finding it as natural an element as walking on the cliffs and across the pasturelands.

One had a picture of a girl remembering little, if anything of her natural mother but growing up in an atmosphere of love, freely bestowed: age eleven when the Great War was declared.

The Isle of Man was isolated, all the peat-cutting concessions on the Beinn-y-phott (peat mount) being taken up by agreed arrangement with the owner of Glen Roy. As in Ireland, fairies were busy taking over deserted cottages, left derelict and never demolished as their owners went to war and did not all return.

'Life was middling,' as the Manxman will say rather than committing himself to a more direct 'good' or 'bad'. Farm stocks of pigs—'Purrs'—roamed wild up on South Barrule. Fishermen gazed anxiously ahead for first sight of the Hill of the Rising Sun (the Western Highlands and Cronk-hy-Irey-Lhaa) so that they might quickly put into port as the rays appeared over the Cliff Peak: safe for the time being from the U-Boats and the mines. The Dracadenias (so-called palms), the Veronicas, olearios, escallionias, camellias and magnolias flourished as in days of peace.

Remote—yet unavoidably involved, as the lists of names on the war memorials of town and village came to show. Among those 'Fallen in Honour' was Jarlath Kermode.

PART 3

GABRIELLE KERMODE

'So you have brought the Cushing saga up as far as the Great War, Mr. Wickham?' Miss Quinn's eyes held a certain amusement as she added her congratulations.

I suppose my enthusiasm was a little hard to explain: to anyone who had not seen Lavinia's portrait, that was. All authorship embodies elements of detection, though this need not imply the writing of 'whodunits'.

Miss Quinn had found out for me that Jarlath had been serving in 'Q' ships: those apparently innocuous yet armed trawlers and similar craft which patrolled home waters in disguise to fool the Hun. Records were naturally kept as to how local men met their end by enemy action. Jarlath's ship had been sunk off Dover, the grave of many brave volunteers.

She could not enlighten me as to who the young fellow with the pale legs might be on the Calf of Man, though she said that she had an idea who it *might* be, which was not precisely the same thing.

'I'd hazard a guess that he is Gabrielle's grandson.'

The elegant coffee tray was beside her and she poured me out a second cup.

'Gabrielle Kermode grew up in Port St. Mary. I fancy her step-mother looked after her until she herself died. She was older than Jarlath, you know.'

I nodded.

The girl had grown up into the 1920's, and married a fisherman who served in the lifeboat crew.

She left Port St. Mary to move the few miles over to Port Erin, to my mind the most attractive of the small resorts on the island. Gabrielle became Mrs Martin Quale and supplemented her young husband's earnings with the trawling fleet by taking summer visitors into their house on the upper tier of the town though still but a few minutes from the sea.

In view of Sir Justin Hardcastle's kindness and shared interest in the Cushing dynasty it had seemed fair to keep him up-to-date with my findings and he wrote, congratulating me upon these modest achievements:

I find the serial a regular cliff-hanging story—Cliff-hanging is the right term, I believe? Our theory about hubris certainly seems to be borne out so far. The death of Arabella's husband almost repeats the Davage pattern. However I do beg leave to doubt her own death by broken heart alone and incline to the view of some organic cause, possibly malnutrition...

It will be most interesting to know what you are able to unearth about the succeeding generation.

I registered some Hall Caine manuscript to my splendid Mrs. T, who must be wondering at the length of my sojourn over in Man, since I had expected to have made it but a few days, with a possible return visit later in the year. Conscience somewhat lightened by this duty done I took myself off to the office of the *Isle of Man Times* and beginning the search through the files from 1925, glancing in passing at an account of the 6th August Flag Day exercise (1927) when the Port St. Mary coxswain was killed by the explosion of the maroon he fired, and a picture of the annual Ascension Day procession from the village club at Andreas.

Newspaper files are like looking through the dictionary in as much as one is always being beguiled away from the object of one's search. However my time was not entirely wasted. Amongst the treasures was a lifeboat crew group which enabled me to pick out Martin Quayle. He looked sturdy, with blond hair and an open smile; stared straight at the photographer. True there was nothing exactly unique about the man who might have been any of half a dozen I had seen in various

parts of the island. There was a wedding day group from 1929, showing Quayle stiff and a little uneasy-looking in what was evidently his Sunday suit. He held his bride's arm very firmly and his buttonhole was almost cabbage-large. The ladies styles of the day look unbelievably comic now, with their oddly-placed waistlines and short skirts—well maybe the hemlengths were quite topical. Gabrielle, seen in her going-away outfit, had a flower pot hat well down on the ears hiding most of her face. Her dark hair was short but there was no way of telling whether it were Eton crop, shingle, or bob with a 'bang' across the forehead. In figure she appeared petite though her husband may have been on the tall side. They were taken outside the church, some even stiffer bridesmaids at their side.
Quaint and rather endearing.

There was nothing else relevant except a picture of the annual angling festival of September with Martin among the competitors. Instructions were certainly strict. Tackle must be 'rod, reel and running line' with a maximum three hooks or one triangle. No fish might be landed by 'hand-lining' but netting and gaffing were permissible. Drifters of the *Manx Fairy* class might cost in the region of £8,000.

'Mr. Quayle of Port Erin with his catch of the day, was the caption under his photo.

I alas am no angler so cannot hazard a hint of what it was he held up with proper pride.

Thanking the people at the newspaper offices I took myself off to one of the cafés for tea and decided that there would be time to write to my parents between this and dinner. My father was going on very well after his heart-attack and I confess to being lazier than I should about keeping in touch. All too easy to find it difficult—once one has left home.

Confirmation rather than advancement and still quite a period of time to be covered. 1929 to 1966, in fact: just three short of forty years. Gabrielle, assuming that she was still alive, would be a woman in her sixties. No great age. Had the family pattern of fatality touched her too? Or had she been allowed to live out her life in quiet normality?

The little guest house had been but a beginning. Within five years the Martin Quayles had left Port Erin for the mainland where they—or possibly just Gabrielle—felt there would be greater opportunity to make money. One cannot blame the young woman for wishing to avoid the drabness she must have associated with her mother's years on the island. At this point all contact with the family ceased until the Second World War brought Gabrielle back with her fraternal twins, descendants maybe of that Geoffrey Quayle who had run a bank—one of the very first—up to 1817! Anyway Gabrielle's sons had gone to King William College, Castletown, becoming prepositors (prefects) and wearing those short gowns which were similar to our commoners' ones at Oxford and 'the other place'. This scholastic side of Quayle life was easy to verify by a visit to the college, which I found impressive.

The Quayle boys had done well, though not brilliantly.

Their father had gone into the Merchant Navy and despite being torpedoed twice and spending hours in rubber dinghies, had returned to his family with no worse than the loss of an arm. No worse? Of course to a fisherman this could prove a severe handicap, even making his normal form of livelihood impossible. Gabrielle appears to have worked in a shop during those years, living in one of Castletown's back streets in order to be near her boys.

The Isle of Man must have been a curious place in World War II, with its huge internment camp of foreigners from England. One imagined famous pianists and international singers cooped up with little East End Jewish tailors, recent escapes from the European pogroms and English people who just happened to have married enemy aliens. I knew that Knockaloe had been a German P.O.W. Camp from 1914-18 and was now an Experimental Farm but where exactly the 1939-1946 civilian detainees had been housed, I did not enquire since it hardly concerned the Quayles.

Taking V.J. day as the true end of the war, the twins would have been sixteen and after a year or so made off to the mainland where opportunities may have seemed to them in turn to be better ...

So I had brought 'the Cushing dynasty' story roughly up to 1948 or 1950 and it began to strike me how little I still knew of them as *people*. Oh, there were facts; quite a bit of background information, together with some hearsay and a mighty lot of guesswork. What had the principal protagonists really been like?

Lavinia I felt I knew the most about, because the portrait had told me a lot more than mere reportage could. Charlotte—for some reason not altogether clear to me—seemed less interesting. Was it just because she had settled down and married a farmer? Her daughter Arabella had begun by seeming adventuresome. At least she had left Lancashire to visit the Isle of Man and met her romantic fate. For all the tragedy of young widowhood I had little impression of anything beyond a somewhat nebulous being, flitting quietly around Port St. Mary and accepting death with a sob of thankfulness. No photographs were made available to help in picturing her. What local friends she may have had, I did not happen to find.

Now Gabrielle surely was more promising. She might still be *alive* and if she was, I intended to find out for myself. (That ridiculous press photo from 1929 was worse than useless!)

The scene of enquiry shifted to Castletown, probably the oldest and most interesting place on the island, dominated as it was by the fortress of Castle Rushen where a browse round gave the chance to study fascinating lists of old penal offences and their often surprisingly stringent punishments.

There was a nautical museum housing the schooner *Peggy* (built and sailed by a Capt. George Quayle in 1789), 40 foot long and walled-in just above the harbour. Within a short distance of the town could be found an 8th century farm, the Golf Links Hotel (reputedly the best tea on Man. Who was I to argue?) and Derby Haven, the sands whereon the first Derby of all had been run in 1630. True it was called the East Derby and raced over a piece of Langness.

Though gambling on horses and dogs was illegal, the betting instinct proved hard to eliminate.

'Wedding days used to be great occasions for holding races,' the custodian on duty at Castle Rushen had told me. 'Men used to take horses to the church, tethering them to the rails and at the end of the wedding service raced to the bride's home. First to arrive could break the wedding cake over her head as she entered!'

'Just a piece—or enough to stun her, do you mean?'

He was unsure and annoyingly could not give any actual instances of this rather barbaric bucolic custom taking place.

'The sort of thing Roger Kermode would have enjoyed' I thought to myself on leaving.

Neither would I have dreamed of missing the witches 'museum' in the Old Mill a little outside Castletown. The collection was remarkably comprehensive, ranging from charms to black magic; dealt with local witches and others, everything carefully documented but so atmospherically lighted as to prove difficult for reading. There was the Red Lady of Garraghan 'often seen on lonely nights' wearing the Welsh steeple hat and red cloak of tradition. In common with most weird sisters she was a signal for ill-luck, and it was said to have been within living memory that Manx farmers drove cattle into the street as protection against the evil eye.

The evil eye! It was almost as if it had followed the families of Cushing and Kermode. When Gabrielle changed her name to Quayle maybe the bad luck had been broken. But of course I was far from knowing the end of her story.

Now old long-established looking shops are often excellent places in which to indulge in fruitful gossip and after a little search I found just the right sort of place and the lady behind the Castletown counter not only willing but pleased to talk. After all it was a miserable, windy sort of morning and myself the only customer. Why else should I have been greeted with such eagerness? Having talked of this and that and made a small purchase I brought conversation round to Gabrielle.

'Mrs. Martin Quayle? Yes, I remember her and the two boys. Nat and Bat they used to be called.'

Nathaniel and Bartholomew one concluded!

'Before Mr. Quayle came back after hostilities—' In London the shopkeeper most likely would have said 'returned to Civvie Street'. 'They had had a daughter. Pretty little thing she was too. Lavinia.'

Lavinia! Let me see now, what relation would the first Lavinia have been to the third? Was there such a thing as a great great aunt?

'Born around nineteen forty two or three I think,' the old lady was recalling.

'What became of the family after the war? I understood Martin Quayle lost an arm. Must have made life a bit difficult. From the deep sea fishing point of view, I mean.'

Gabrielle, faced with a husband unlikely to be able to work in his old line, had returned to the obvious, taking in summer visitors. Martin's gratuity went into a small guest house concern in Douglas, where opportunity doubtless was best. Together they worked this up into a going concern. One knew the sort of thing: good breakfast, main meal of the day at 5 p.m. and a supper around 9 p.m.

'Nat and Bat went to the mainland.'—I nodded—'Nat married pretty early. A Blackpool young lady. I did hear it's their son who's out on the Calf for the summer. Training to be an ornithologist.'

Marvellous woman! She did not even hesitate over the word!

Dear Miss Quinn had been perfectly right as to the identity of the pale-legged youth whom I had seen. It would be interesting to arrange a meeting between us but the question was—how?—with the Calf closed to the public until long after I should have returned to London. I stilled the inner voice whispering 'But you could come back again in August. He'll probably still be there then.'

'What about the other twin? Bat, as you called him?'

The woman's face took on a sad expression and instinctively I steeled myself for another family tragedy. Bat had been 'mad on motor cycles', as were so many of his and the succeeding generation. What more natural than that he should wish to compete in the Manx cycle races?

'He'd done quite a bit already so I did hear.'

Everyone visiting Man was more or less bound to have driven over all or most of the celebrated T.T. course. Whilst I had missed the actual race on my arrival, I had found the stands along the mainroad out of Douglas still in erection and sandbagged corners in various places. Enthusiasts from all over the world entered and sidecar and motor scooter races had been added to the annual list of events.

The actual T.T. course had to be covered seven times, averaging 90 m.p.h. The start down Bray Hill was taken at around 129 m.p.h. slowing to 85 m.p.h. at Union Mills.

'The tricky corners are Greeba Bridge and Ballacraine Hotel.'

The Laurel Bank was best done at 60-80 m.p.h.: the down-hill bend at the 11th milestone usually at 120.

'Would that be the fastest lap?' I interrupted her commentary, having the normal mechanically-minded male interest in such details. Apparently not. 130 m.p.h. was considered 'feasible' for the 13th milestone section, dropping to a cautious 75-80 for the hump-backed bridge at Ballaugh. Here machines literally left the ground: 'two point landing' being essential. Quarry Bend curves at 100 m.p.h., Ginger Hill 70, remembering to lift the head at an unnatural angle to miss the telegraph post ahead.

Here it was that Bartholomew Quayle misjudged things. Ironically enough the final portion via Ramsey and Gooseneck was comparatively innocuous, not forgetting the hairpin at Governor's Bridge.

'Was young Quayle killed?' The question seemed—well—superfluous.

'Outright. His parents never felt the same about the island after that. Sort of lost interest in their guest house, I understand.'

By 1957 it had run into difficulties. In 1958 it closed.

'I'm afraid I couldn't tell you what became of them after that but I daresay you could make enquiries in Douglas.'

Which was precisely what I intended to do.

2

Country bus services have an enchanting propensity to be tours around the intermediate villages—enchanting, that was, if the traveller were not in any hurry. The Isle of Man Road Services were no different and a half hour's car run of the 16 miles from Douglas to Port Erin would be a good hour's trip by public transport. Returning to Ramsey from Castlehaven was quicker. Pleased as I was with my afternoon's findings in the old capital I knew that I had an appointment over at Manghold in the morning with regard to the Hall Caine material: this must not be shirked since some trouble had been involved in the fixing. Whilst there I intended to walk out onto the headland, none of my previous visits having permitted time to do this. There were disadvantages about not having a car. Hiring was expensive and my engagements had to fit in with road and rail itineraries.

When I reached my hotel I found a message in the rack. It was from Miss Quinn, asking me to coffee next evening:

> *There is someone whom I'm sure you'll be interested to meet coming so I do hope you'll be free.*

Miss Quinn's calligraphy was remarkably difficult to disentangle but by this time I had learned that sudden assault was more likely to reveal the meaning than any prolonged close study. (Those who did the typing of her learned articles and papers were to be pitied.) Still I had become fairly proficient at deciphering her by this time and rang through graciously accepting. Efforts to find out who the fellow guest was to be were unavailing.

'Tut, tut, Mr. Wickham! Do you want to spoil my little surprise?' Her tone was positively roguish.

Turning it over in my mind before joining Mr. Potts for what would, in fact, be our last pre-dinner drink together—the habit of assembling for one had developed before I so much as noticed its regularity—I assumed that Miss Quinn was entertaining some academic friend or else a fellow author. She might consider that either would be of interest to me but there was not, one would have thought, any reason for such amused secrecy on her part.

'Had a good day, Wickham?' Little Mr. Potts beamed, as he awaited me. 'I told you the sun would come out after lunch, didn't I?'

Had he? I expect so, but the weather had never been that important, except when I had nothing with which to occupy myself. The Mermaid Bar—actually mermaids were supposed to frequent Garwick Bay on the other side of the island—was modern with suitably piscatorial murals and a kind of underwater tinge to the decor in general. I did not greatly care for all this, I must admit, still it was popular with most of the guests.

'Your usual?' I asked Potts, having moved up to the bar counter to order. He nodded and I carried our drinks over to one of the small tables, helping myself to an olive after laying down the tray. He enquired about the sort of day I had had. As usual, he himself had been out on a boat trip. This prompted me to ask:

'Have you heard of the odd local superstition about the third boat out being unlucky?'

'Oh, yes.'

'Do you imagine there's any truth in the idea?'

'Ask Raymond'—one of the Ramsey longshoremen.

We agreed that most superstitions had a basis of fact, though often quite a tenuous one and how the majority of legends and stories grew 'better' with repetition.

'I've never actually been here to see the fishing boats go out to sea,' Mr. Potts acknowledged, though he had watched the lifeboat being launched on more than one occasion. 'I'd help, if I were a bit younger.'

He was one of those men whom it would be difficult to classify as regards age but may well have been considerably older than his mini-Pickwickian appearance suggested. He had been coming to the island for a good many years.

'I've travelled a lot in my day, you know, but I find it suits me here as well as anywhere. There was quite a swell at sea this morning. Just how I like it!'

He had been to the Calf again: his pet trip.

'Anyone seasick?' I asked, having been told repeatedly that he himself was impervious.

'Very nearly. She was leaning over the side. *Said* she was looking for *Cughtagh*.'

'Come again?'

'*Cughtagh*. He's a sea monster whose breathing can be heard in caves even on calm days—and today wasn't calm!'

We laughed. On this occasion there had been neither mail nor provisions to deliver: Mr. Potts was doubtful they could have gone in close enough to do this. The boat had kept further out than it usually did which prevented seeing the rocks from the best position.

Dinner was about to be served so we drank up and went in, taking coffee afterwards in the lounge. Mr. Potts and most of the others went to look at television and I to write up Hall Caine notes and prepare what would be wanted for my morning appointment . . .

It was Saturday and quite a few people were down for very

early breakfast in order to catch the 9 o'clock boat from Douglas back to Liverpool. Funny Mr. Potts himself was going and in an odd sort of way I should miss him.

My morning's work proved useful rather than exciting and I did a small circuit of places connected with Hall Caine before relaxing over a Tyrolean tea at the flourishing cafe in Laxey Glen. It was very like the real thing and afforded pleasant memories of the past. In fact I sent my parents a card of the place as a reminder of the first 'abroad' holiday for the three of us after the war.

A clean shirt and my better suit seemed indicated for Miss Quinn. I went in promptly to dinner, which sometimes was a little slow in service, and at eight o'clock presented myself yet again at Mona Villa. Blanche Quinn greeted me in her usual welcoming manner and announced that the other guest had not yet arrived.

'Male or female?'

'I'm not telling you a single thing in advance, Mr. Wickham! And while we are waiting—tell me about this morning.'

Having been instrumental in fixing the appointment in the first place, Miss Quinn was naturally anxious to receive a progress report. Some rather pleasant music was coming over the wireless and we broke off to listen to the announcer's identification of the piece. It turned out to be Haydn Wood's Manx Rhapsody.

'Was he a Manxman then?' displaying my ignorance of most matters musical.

'Indeed he was and proud of the fact, as he should be.'

'You knew him?'

'Slightly. A funny little man. Somewhat shy but endearing. I remember him saying that his head was full of nothing much except tunes. He was a fine violinist, of course and his wife a singer. A statuesque woman, as I recall her. They used to do a turn together on the music halls.' Miss Quinn paused. 'I fancy Haydn half regretted the immense popularity of "Roses of Picardy" though I believe it put him near the millionaire class at the time. He was a little sad at being labelled "Light" music.'

'Wasn't Arthur Sullivan always longing to compose grand opera instead of the Savoy ones?'

'I think Haydn also would have liked to do a really big work ... certainly to have been remembered by something other than his popular ballads. He was a very keen bridge player, too.'

Music and bridge? Well, why ever not!

At that moment the bell sounded. Miss Quinn's face assumed a highly mischievous expression as we rose to greet the visitor.

'Miss Lavinia Quayle,' the little maid announced.

I must have looked incredibly foolish, standing jaw a-gape and, for aught I know, eyes-a-pop. For there before me, allowing for the changes of period and hair-style, was a young woman who could so easily have stepped straight out of that portrait of Lavinia Cushing! There was the same straight glance, the little arrogant lift to the chin, the very expression of the face. However, instead of the beautiful silk dress which the almost unknown artist had captured with such perfection, she wore a plain modern frock that could serve equally well for a cocktail party or informal dinner. She advanced towards me with a quick, easy walk: in fact exactly the way I had imagined she would move. Hers was a neatly fashioned body.

'Mr. Wickham? I believe you profess an interest in our dark family secrets! I can't imagine why!' and she laughed, displaying even teeth. Her voice was deeper than expected and wonderfully warm. The kind novelists of the 1930's described as being 'dark brown'.

All I could do was to stand and blurt out 'Lavinia Cushing!'

She looked at me as if I were very slightly mad, for which I am sure I do not blame her. She frowned, trying to puzzle things out:

'Lavinia Cushing? Why she lived ages ago! Way back in the eighteen fifties or something like that.'

'Yes, but then you see the resemblance between you is amazing. If you were dressed in the period I would have said that you *were* Lavinia Cushing instead of just named after her.'

'I'm not sure you're quite right about that. I imagine my parents just hit on the name and liked it.' Her manner did not suggest any personal affection for Lavinia. 'But how is it you know how my ancestor looked? I mean there weren't photographs in those days, were there?'

Here Miss Quinn intervened, explaining about the Ambrose Keeling portrait up at Cartmel. 'I have an idea Mr. Wickham quite fell in love with Lavinia Cushing!'

The tone was teasing nevertheless it caused me to flush up as if I were a schoolboy and Miss Quayle continued to look entirely bewildered.

Normality was restored by the arrival of coffee. Lavinia was still looking at me as if my face could reveal some riddle for her. At length her puzzled expression cleared. She said she believed that there had been a portrait of her ancestor.

'I've never seen it, mind, but heard about it in an indirect sort of way. I haven't the faintest idea what relation to me this Lavinia Cushing would be.'

I confessed the nearest I had managed was great great aunt. 'It really needs a genealogical tree to make the whole thing clear.'

'I wonder how the portrait came to leave your family?' Miss Quinn asked, having reached the last of our three cups.

'Oh, that's easy. I expect it was sold. I can't say that I ever remember being told how or when!' She turned her head in my direction. 'It doesn't sound the sort of thing one would hang up in a guest house!'

'Keeling's portrait is a very fine piece of work, Miss Quayle.'
'That's what I meant. *Too* fine!'

'I can see you two are going to have heaps to talk about,' Miss Quinn observed, indicating that I was to see to the drinks as had been customary on previous visits. Miss Quinn herself invariably had a small cognac.

'Miss Quayle?'

She gave the several attractively coloured bottles her serious study before selecting cherry brandy, in which I joined her, aware of Miss Quinn's amusement since I was accustomed to taking a drambui. She addressed Lavinia.

'As I was telling you on the telephone yesterday, Mr. Wickham seems to have an insatiable interest in what he calls the Cushing dynasty.'

'Then you probably know more about the past of my family than I do myself. Oh, I have a vague idea the Cushings lived in Lancs and that Lavinia was killed by her outraged husband.'

I volunteered to fill in a few more details and did so at her invitation. When I had finished she made a dry little comment:

'That nineteenth century Lavinia was a bit of a *femme fatale* wouldn't you say?'

'I hope you also aren't going to be haunted by the family's ill-luck, Miss Quayle.'

'Frankly I've never thought about fate, as such. Would you say we have been especially unlucky then?'

'Up to now it does seem as if a certain pattern of tragedy was repeating itself down the generations.' This from Blanche Quinn.

'I'll agree about the Cushings, though didn't Charlotte just marry a farmer and lead a pretty normal sort of life? A baby dying in infancy in *those* days wasn't all that remarkable and I suppose people are still gored by bulls if they work on the land.'

I was not giving in quite so easily as that and asked:

'What about the Kermodes? Would you call their record humdrum?'

'Grandma's husband falling into the harbour and being killed, you mean? That *was* sad and—it's always seemed to me—pretty unnecessary.'

'According to locals she died of a broken heart.'

'Really Mr. Wickham! Hasn't it occurred to you that they were pulling your leg? Dying of love indeed!'.

'Some people—' but her laughter made it impossible for me to sound serious any longer.

'Miss Quayle has a dispassionate and at the same time a very logical mind, you must agree,' Miss Quinn's tone was meant to tantalise. 'You, Mr. Wickham, are apt to regard facts a little too romantically, as is common amongst writers of fiction. You know *my* view. That the woman starved herself. Maybe deliberately, maybe not.'

Lavinia had lighted a cigarette but after a puff or two laid it beside her on the ashtray. 'Mother hardly remembered grandma. At least she's seldom spoken about her, though I've heard lots about Jarlath. He sounded a nice person.' The tone implied 'a my-sort-of-person'. Quickly her glance challenged me. 'I suppose you regard his being killed in the war as a further manifestation or—whatever you call it—'

'*Hubris*.' Miss Quinn's prompt was softly made.

The girl frowned. 'I'd simply call it sheer bad luck. In any case weren't the casualties in the First World War simply terrific?' I nodded and we discussed the various battles we had read about.

People kept early hours in Ramsey and we all seemed to have talked a lot. Nevertheless it came as an unpleasant shock to find it just on eleven. As guests we rose simultaneously to say goodnight to Miss Quinn. Outside her house I asked:

'May I walk you to wherever it is you're staying, Miss Quayle?'

She smiled, indicating a pale blue mini on the corner, confiding that she disliked Ramsey and had a pet pub down Kirk Michael way.

'You wouldn't like me to drop you instead, Mr. Wickham?'

I explained that this was entirely unnecessary as my hotel was but five minutes walk from Mona Villa. The thought of Lavinia driving out of my life again, perhaps for good, was more than I could bear so I heard myself asking if she were over for long.

'Really I'm here to look up Gordy.'

This was Pale-legs and, absurd though it must seem, her nephew. She herself was no more than twenty-two or three and he was probably between seventeen and eighteen. Still I recollected that Nat Quayle was born before the war and had married young.

'Are you expecting to spend all your time with him?'

'You're being very transparent, Mr. Wickham! No of course not. He's on the Calf to do a job of study. I'm just hoping for half a day in his company.'

'When can I see you again?'

'I know Gordy's tied up all tomorrow.'

'In that case may I give you lunch somewhere?'

She hesitated, then saying that as she had a car, might not a drive first be an idea? She expected that she could find somewhere I had not been already.

'That sounds marvellous.'

We fixed the details, liable to be changed if the day proved to be wet, but judging by the night's clear sky it ought to be fine.

'Au revoir, Mr. Wickham,' and she held out a small, firm hand. We stood looking at one another for a long minute before she made any move towards her car.

PART 4

LAVINIA QUAYLE

I

There can be no explanation for the sense of expectancy with which I rose on the following morning. After all it was hardly the first time that I should be spending several hours in the society of an attractive girl. And she was attractive, though it would be difficult to say in just what way. There was such a warmth and friendliness about her, too. Of course it was stupid to be influenced by some trick of heredity which made her resemblance so startlingly a woman who had lived more than a hundred years earlier. Besides one could not know with what degree of accuracy Ambrose Keeling had painted his beloved, or how good a likeness the portrait was. Might it not have been a highly imaginative piece of work rather than a definite copying of the Cushing physiognomy?. And yet one knew instinctively that the picture was good. To pretend that Miss Quayle was a kind of reincarnation of an earlier Lavinia was absurd. This I recognised. Still there was this quite extraordinary resemblance which no one probably could explain in everyday terms.

From the wide dining room windows at breakfast-time the sea mist seemed promising to lift within a little while and a day with that start could change completely by noon. In fact such were the peculiarities of the island climate that it might be raining hard in Douglas but sunny in Peel.

The pale blue mini drew up at the time arranged, watched by me from the lounge, which overlooked the entrance. She closed the car door and hurried into the hotel. Not wishing to appear foolishly eager, I let her enquire for me at the reception desk.

'Mr. Wickham, please.'

The youth on duty came to find me.

Lavinia's red hair was set in slight waves which fell to her shoulders. She wore a light summer two-piece, paler than the deep blue of her eyes and sensible sandals—not the type just kept in place by a thong between the toes.

'I have several places in mind,' she announced, as we went out together to the car. 'But of course I don't know exactly where you will have been—apart from the Caine country of course,' her eyes twinkled. 'How is the book going, by the way?'

My reply was a little too evasive to satisfy her. She accused me of faintheart then her manner softened and she said she did not altogether blame me.

'We did Hall Caine at school and at his most ranting he is a bit of an old bore. Have you read *all* his books, Mr Wickham?'

'Couldn't we make it Jake?'

'As you wish! I don't have to tell you my Christian name, do I? Friends and family shorten it to Vinia. My enemies, and people who wish to annoy me, make it Lavvy.' She smiled again, still not starting the car. 'You can imagine what fun that was at school.'

Becoming business-like she put me through a quick topographical examination. Had I seen the hill near Tynwald where witches used to be rolled down in barrels which contained protruding nails on the inside?

'The Manx are a humane people, you see, and didn't go much on burning their witches.'

I was not sure that the alternative was particularly humane and said so. She did not argue the point.

'Well, it's just a hill. Perhaps not worth bothering about really. You'll have been through Colby, of course? But did you see the Archibald Cregeen house near there?'

'The gentleman who spent thirty years compiling a Manx dictionary? Yes I did.'

'He was a remarkable man, considering that he was entirely

98

self-educated. He was also Coroner of Rushen sheading.' (The island was divided up into six sheadings, or districts, and the four main townsteads.)

To Lavinia's disappointment I had also discovered for my-self the Nunnery where a Subaltern Fry fell in love with an heiress and became one of the island Governors. But Kentrough I did not know and we drove straight to this family house which, according to Lavinia, at one time had both its own brewery and private bank, not to mention an early form of icebox. She pointed out the inscription over the gate:

Judge not your fellow man's condition, until you be in his position.

'I must say that it's a lot more agreeable being shown places by someone who knows the island as intimately as you do, Vinia.'

'But I don't! Not really. I mean, we didn't move around much when we lived here.'

'I know very little about your side of the family.'

She made a face at me. 'It's too early in the day for reminiscing! Our next objective is Arbory. There's the church and you might as well have a look at Quilliam's grave. After all, he was steersman of the *Victory*. Also Arbory is interesting because it is there that the last parish fair is kept up. It's called Laa Columb Killey. Actually it's a flower and vegetable affair, complete with kiddies' parade, sports and sideshows.'

'I'd like to be here when they hold it one year.'

Having done our duty by the village of Arbory she drove me right up to Injebreck, which was not only in the beautiful mountainous region of the island but had a reservoir attractive in its way as the famous Rhayader dams of Wales.

'Three hundred million gallons of water, Jake!'

'The mind boggles at such figures! When was this reservoir made? Would you have any idea?'

'1905. All right! I *did* look it up before coming out!'

We had a drink in this area. (It was early for lunch.) And at last Lavinia began to speak of her childhood. Her two brothers Nat and Bat were twelve when she was born and looked upon as 'exalted beings' from high-chair level, which was how she put it.

'They were amused by suddenly having a baby sister. I could not be expected to be any sort of companion to them, of course, but they were awfully good and patient with me. In a silly sort of way I suppose I worshipped them—particularly Bat.'

'He was the one who was killed in the T.T. races?'

She nodded, making no attempt to hide the tears that gushed into her eyes. 'That was the most awful day in the whole of my life. You see, I was there—watching.'

'Oh, my God.'

'So were our parents. You have seen the map of the course? Therefore you know the hazards.'

'They have been explained to me.'

'Bat had been over the course lots of times. Most local boys have. He was a fine rider, make no mistake about that.'

'It is still possible to misjudge things.'

'He didn't,' she protested. 'Heavens, Jake, he could have ridden blindfold over the course—well, almost. Anyway, they were past the two-point landing of Quarry Bend without mishap, and coming towards Ginger Hill, where it is necessary to drop speed. Bat was lying second and his chances were good. Suddenly the chap immediately in front lost control. I fancy it was a tyre burst or something to do with his steering. Anyway he skidded violently and Bat couldn't pull up in time. He—he hit the telegraph pole.'

The one just past the corner...

Lavinia shuddered at the memory and the expression in her eyes was that of a frightened child. Instinctively I laid my hand on hers, but doubt that she noticed.

'Try not to think about it,' I urged.

As if I were not even there she said that her brother had broken his neck and must have died instantly.

100

'Mother took it the worst. I suppose Father realised there couldn't have been any hope.'

From what Lavinia told me that day—and later—the decline in Quayle fortunes could be dated from the time of Bat's death. They ran into increasing financial difficulties. There was no denying that Gabrielle had brooded over her son's death to the extent of neglecting everything except the upkeep of her own sorrow. Martin had done his one-armed best to run the guest house almost unaided. Though his wife still cooked, she took little trouble. Meals became dull and tasteless. She presented what Lavinia called 'a closed face' to the holiday makers who booked up with them and that was not what people liked. In the end the Quayles were sold up and the guest house passed into different hands.

'My elder brother Nat—well he was the senior twin by about half an hour—went in for motor engineering when he left the island.'

The brothers appeared to have been very different in their ideas and ambitions. Nat was the steady one who knew exactly what he wanted to do in life. Bat had been restless and seeking.

'You know the way it is, Jake. One minute he talked about going to sea.'

'With your ancestry that would seem a logical career for him to choose.'

'Oh, he didn't want to trawl. Neither did he relish going into the Merchant Navy, starting at the bottom. His idea was to become an artificer.'

One gathered either that the training was too arduous or expensive. Bat drifted from one job to another, working for a time under his brother in the Midlands.

'Nat married when he was only eighteen, you know,' Lavinia continued telling me, over a second drink.

'Well I gathered something of the sort since he has a son. This Gordy, you call him.'

She smiled. 'Gordy's a nice person. Very staid and serious.

Not a bit like me! He's only six years younger than I am. Absurd, isn't it?'

'And is Nat happily married?'

'Most. They have a nice bungalow on one of the new housing estates near the works. Northants isn't to be compared to the island, of course, but it could be worse. As a matter of fact I've been staying with them for a few days.'

I did not know where she normally lived and it came as a pleasant surprise to learn that she was domiciled in London.

'Where else?' and she laughed, encouraging me to talk about the estimable Mrs. T and the digs where I lived. She told me she couldn't afford a flat on her own, so she shared one with three girls in Putney.

'You know what *that* means—washing up, bed making, trips to the laundrette.' She raised her chin and for a moment was once again the Lavinia of the portrait. 'Delia—one of the girls, leaves to get married in two weeks time so we shall be on the look out for another to join us, and it helps if we all get on!'

'What sort of job do you do?'

She was with a travel agency: purveyor of package tours to romantic places. There were fare concessions which was how she managed to come popping over to the island for a long weekend.

'Is that all?' The dismay in my voice must have been obvious.

'Well this time, yes. The car isn't mine, you know. It's just loaned me by a friend.'

Male or female? Ridiculous how jealous I was beginning to feel! Still if the colour of the borrowed car was any guide then it was a girl friend.

We drove back past the reservoir to Baldwin and via Cronk Ny Mucaillyn past Crosby and the Highlander Inn, then pausing at Glenfaba Bridge in order that Lavinia might point out two different types of masonry. The river which the bridge spanned marked the boundary between a pair of parishes, each with its own highway authority so, in the Irish manner,

Patrick and its neighbour on the opposite side of the bridge, built half each.

'The Battle of Santwat took place here in the eleventh century, Jake. The southern factions were led by one Macmarus and the north by some earl whose name I forget. The north were winning hands down when the southern women swept from the slopes where they had been watching the combat. Their fighting was so furious that they won the day for their side. And do you know what? According to Manx tradition over the centuries the women from the south of the island have a special reward.'

'Which is?'

'When their husband dies they receive half his estate. Whereas if they are from the north, they're only entitled to a third!'

'Lucky your grandmother Arabella lived at Port St. Mary then.'

'Oh, but she wasn't a true islander. She only came on a visit and stayed to marry my grandfather, Gabriel Kermode. If you ask me, I'd say she received nothing at all!'

'It's a pretty fable about the bridge and now, young lady, where do you suggest that I take you for lunch?'

We decided to make for Peel.

Over our meal she entertained me with an account of what took place on St. Stephen's Day. 'It's called "Hunting the wren" and I believe my brothers were roped in as children.'

'What happens exactly?'

'The boys procesh—if there's any such word—from house to house carrying a basket decorated with feathers.'

There were also wooden hoops festooned with ribbons and streamers containing a decorated cushion.

'They sing a silly sort of song. "We'll away to the wood says Robin to Bobbin," repeat "Dickin to Robin" then "Jacko o' the land" and finally "everyone". I believe in the old days a wren actually was hunted and killed, its feathers being sold as charms.'

'Nowadays all the folk melodies seem to be songs of protest in one form or another.'

'They aren't true folk tunes, are they? Just—well—I call them bandwagon ballads!'

I laughed for Lavinia was indeed an entertaining companion. She told me that she would be spending as much of next day as she could with young Gordon and commended me again to my Caine researches. I made a face of reproach, indicating a far greater interest in 'the Cushing dynasty'.

'Surely you know enough about us by this time?' She gave a provocative smile.

'Not nearly. I'm avid for further information.'

'Such as?'

'When I'm to have the pleasure of seeing you again.'

'Is it such a pleasure, Jake?'

'Yes.'

There must have been a sincerity in my utterance that touched her for she laid a hand on my forearm as we drove back to Ramsey at the end of our day. 'I'd like that enormously, Jake. I don't imagine that Gordy will be able to have additional time off. Saturday is his usual free day.'

'What exactly does he do on the Calf? Bird watch?'

'I imagine so. He's very—dedicated.' There was affectionate raillery in her manner. One could tell that she and the pale-legged boy were attached. Perhaps there was something about him which reminded her of her dead brother? How alike had the Quayle twins been—in looks? To wonder, to was to ask. She considered a moment, explaining—though I knew already—that they were not identical twins. While there was quite a resemblance they were not alike enough for confusion.

'I suppose Gordy is similar to his father in appearance?'

She shook her head. 'Oddly enough he's much closer to Bat. Not only in appearance, but in other things as well. With this one great difference. Gordy knows exactly where he's going in life. I've never come across anyone with so few doubts. Do you have doubts, Jake?'

'Lots. And you?'

She nodded, her expression changing to wistfulness. 'About God and why one is born into this world. Doubts about—oh, lots of things. But you wouldn't want to hear them.'

Actually I would—though this was no time to tell her so.

'I'm extra fond of Gordy because he is so like Bat,' she admitted, adding thoughtfully that it was odd the way one loved certain people so much more than others. 'Nat's a terribly nice person. Far more dependable than darling Bat ever was or I imagine would have become.'

We were following the main road which was also part of the T.T. circuit, passing Drinkwater's corner and going on up towards Handley's corner and Baargaroo Hill.

'Have you ever thought, Vinia, that your twin brothers must have had a good many characteristics in common with Gabriel and Jarlath Kermode? As I understand it, Gabriel was the wild, the careless one and Jarlath—'

'Goody goody! Nat isn't that, thank the Lord. He's pretty average, I'd say, but he hasn't quite the warmth, the quick attraction that was Bat's best weapon in life. Nat's quieter. He's even-tempered and sincere. Oh dear! What a priggish paragon I'm making him sound!'

'You wouldn't have any family photos?'

'I don't travel about with them.'

I realised the question had been a foolish one. If girls carried around photos, then usually they were of the boy friend. I wondered whether Vinia had one but it was much too early to ask. So I said that it was tantalising not knowing how the various people looked. Apart from the Keeling portrait all I had seen of the first Lavinia's descendants was that poorly reproduced wedding photo of Gabrielle and Martin Quayle.

Lavinia chuckled. 'Oh *that*! There used to be an enlargement of the thing on the mantelpiece when we lived in Castletown. I imagine it must be knocking around somewhere though I can't remember seeing it for a very long time.'

I had been brought roughly up to date with the Quayle

family and knew that none of them any longer lived on the island. The parents had settled not far from Nat and his family.

Martin Quayle did odd jobs of one kind and another, but Lavinia was reticent about the way in which Gabrielle filled in her time. They appeared to live in very modest circumstances: a couple of rooms in someone else's house. It occurred to me that Gabrielle also might go out to work. Perhaps it was not of the kind her daughter approved? Be that as it might I had not pressed for information the girl might not wish to give. After all this was still very early in our acquaintance.

By now we had reached Cronk-y-Croghee village just outside Kirk Michael and Lavinia interrupted my thoughts with the information that the Manx name meant 'Hill of Hanging' and was the place of execution for those who had committed offences under ecclesiastical law.

'What a little mine of information you are, to be sure.'

Assuming a virtuous expression she said that she was accustomed to doing her homework.

'Are you dropping in on Miss Quinn again this evening, Jake?'

'I don't think so. Why?'

'Just wondered. You're quite buddies, aren't you?'

'Well we seem to share a number of interests in a semi-academic fashion. She's been most helpful.'

'Over Hall Caine or the Cushing dynasty?'

'Both!'

'Tell me, Jake, are you planning to make a novel out of the family?'

I did not entirely escape that momentary guilt experienced by authors when pressed for their plot and character sources. Perhaps right at the start there had been some such idea, but already it had become impossible. As Anouilh says, in his character as author in *The Cavern*, that was the one play he had never been able to write, because he was too involved. For me, it was a novel.

106

The day ahead seemed a dull, unglamorous thing without Lavinia and I did not go far afield but spent most of the time catching up on work and studying an account of Hall Caine's attitude to religion which Miss Quinn had given me on the previous evening. Anything likely to illuminate this strange, visionary man's character was too precious to ignore. The whole assignment was proving more difficult even than imagined at the start—perhaps because it was impossible to involve myself in the life and work of a person so alien in character to myself. The cool, official re-appraisal would not be sufficient. Somehow I must establish a *rapport* with this man of letters.

'If only I had liked him better either as a person or as a writer.'

Strolling along between the two piers after tea and wondering a little how to occupy myself until such time as I might drop back the article at Miss Quinn's before returning to the hotel to dinner, I came across an ornate notice advertising Mme. Zorah 'up one flight of stairs'. She termed herself variously clairvoyant and palmist. Fortune telling was good fun at any time and while maintaining that I believed in it not at all, I was nevertheless a sucker for cards and crystal ball divination. Logic in this there was none. As a former schoolmaster accustomed to dishing out facts, by rights I should have no truck with the purely fanciful. Still Mme. Zorah did sound an alluring way of idling half an hour.

The initial flight of stairs ended at a door, immediately ahead. The steps then continued upwards. A turnable card with 'engaged' and 'please enter' was displayed on the latter side. No mistake was possible since Mme. Zorah's name was repeated in big black letters on a very off-white door. Oh well, one did not look for pristine freshness in a palmist's domain.

My knock was answered by a gutteral voice saying 'Come!' Opening the door I manoeuvred through one of those coloured plastic strip screens into a semi-darkened room, mysterious lighting being part of the trade. Also it possibly disguised the fact that observed at close quarters, Mme. was wrinkled, with small monkey-brain inquisitive eyes and definite beginnings of a moustache. She wore the popular palmist's attire of coloured kerchief on the head, golden earrings and a dress that passed as Romany. She was more likely to be a diddicoy—that was, not an authentic gipsy but one with the mixed blood of alien races as well.

Our business transaction prearranged, she took my hands, one after the other, studying their backs first then tracing a few lines in the palm with a gilded pencil: all the familiar stuff about health, length of life, number of children to be expected and the various mounts which indicated facets of character.

'Really it is the future I should like to know something about, Mme. Zorah.'

Abruptly her manner changed. Almost apologetically now she explained that she was not supposed to foretell things that might be happening a long way ahead but if I wished she would try to give a lead about one or two *possible* events. Vaguely I recalled that telling the future was not quite legal and so technical evasions may well have been necessary.

There was always a fascination watching someone peer into that crystal ball nestling on its black velvet cushion. For me the same expectant feeling that was aroused when the white ball first began to pop around a roulette wheel.

She began speaking in a sing-song, unnatural voice.

'You are moving into a different phase of your life and I must warn you that there will be elements of danger ahead.'

She went on to say that I had met someone who made a great impression upon me. Vinia! Who else?

Delicately she asked whether she would not be right in thinking that up to now love affairs with women had not played any great part in my life. The remark annoyed me. I had no wish to be taken for a queer so explained coldly that there had been no serious love affair—'Put it that way.'

'I suppose I've been waiting until such time as I meet the right sort of girl.'

'You are romantic. Yes? I think that you *have* met such a girl. And quite recently, too.'

'Perhaps!' Damn it, I was not going to admit as much to Mme. Zorah! Who went on in a more dreamy tone:

'You are on the threshold of a new and profound experience. It could be a love affair ... Certainly I think it is more serious than simple friendship.'

'Could you describe the young woman at all?'

A lot more peering then, half closing her eyes as if conjuring up some vision which I could not share, she gave a marvellously exact description of the portrait in Sir Justin's home: even to the colour of Lavinia Cushing's dress which was described in some detail.

Mme. did not attempt to explain how this woman of another century should have become connected with my life. She accepted the fact.

'This woman I have just described to you was surrounded by tragedy. A tragedy which appears to have been handed on to those who followed her. I think that she died an unnatural death.'

'She was shot by a jealous husband.'

'Ah! Zoh? You are much interested in this person?'

'In her history? Yes, I suppose that I am.'

'The picture reforms and I see a girl who is strangely like the other ...'

The words flowed on hypnotically. At that stage I would have believed any nonsense the woman told me, but it did not seem to be rubbish. Out of a welter of metaphors such as 'surrounded by scorpions' she described Lavinia Quayle almost as accurately as she had the lady of the portrait. Not once but twice I was warned of danger. A danger hard to define.

'It seems to connect with this young girl.'

Inevitably that would be the case.

'Your two lives are moving ever closer—' (I could have hugged Mme. for that!) '—with much happiness comes also great fear. But I think you are strong.'

'Can you tell whether it is the young lady or myself who is most likely to be in danger?'

'I should say both of you.' She pushed the crystal aside, regretting that there was no more to be seen.

Very willingly I paid what she had asked for at the beginning.

'I think you will know happiness in the end,' she called in bright parting accents, leaving me to walk slowly down the steps, wondering how much I ought to believe.

'It's a lot of rot really and yet—' It was that 'and yet' which made me disinclined to dismiss the whole thing as lucky invention. Most likely it had arisen from a clever combination of thought reading and the ability to sum up a stranger by various physical characteristics. Unlike most palmists, however, she had not asked a lot of leading questions: only the month and hour of my birth in order to fix the zodiac and planet signs regulating my destiny.

Miss Quinn was at home when I went round to leave the article and asked me to join her in a sherry before going back to the hotel.

'I'm glad you found this useful, Mr. Wickham,' taking the envelope from me with a smile and going on to ask what I had thought of Miss Quayle.

'A charming girl.'

'And did you spend a nice day together yesterday? Oh come! I was only indulging in a little harmless deduction.'

I gave a brief account of our doings, explaining that it was hoped we might meet again on the morrow.

Miss Quinn had friends in common with Lavinia and it was through them she learned of the girl's pending visit to see Gordy. The arrangements to meet me were not difficult to make. Warmly I said: 'I'm grateful. Truly grateful to you.'

'How solemn you sound, Mr. Wickham.'

'Did I? I didn't mean to,' and I tried to shrug off what seemed too great a revelation of my feelings. Not that I could hope to hide them long from Miss Quinn. For all her air of academic remoteness she was very astute.

'You seem determined to play with fire, my friend.'

'How so?'

'Aren't you forgetting—*hubris*?'

I was not: only trying to convince myself—against more sensible judgement—that there was no truth in the idea of tragedy-haunted families. *All* families had bizarre lapses in fortune and which of us could claim that nothing out of the ordinary had taken place within a generation or two? Had every one of my ancestors lived to a ripe age to die peacefully in bed? Had there been neither madness nor mayhem among past Wickhams? And was one to suppose that all Miss Quinn's forebears had lived as conventional lives as herself? Might there not have been at least one renegade or murderer amongst the past ranks?

'Perhaps we have been making too much of a set of—coincidences, Miss Quinn.'

'That was not the opinion you held a week ago.'

'I agree that it was not. And, to be perfectly honest, it still looks to me as though there have been an unusual number of catastrophes in the family. Surely there is no reason to imagine that Vinia—Miss Quayle, I mean—also is foredoomed?'

'Not unless you believe there is some kind of curse over the Cushings and the generations that followed them. Curses, Mr. Wickham, have to be expiated. By some method or by direct sacrifice to the gods which govern our fate.'

The idea that Lavinia could be in danger of a quite unknown type was worrying. It was easy to dismiss all the things that had befallen the families concerned as ill-luck. A sort of being in the right place only at the wrong time. Perhaps on a different day the Cushings need never have been drowned in their attempt to cross the sands of Morecambe Bay. The fog might not have come up at all; in which case the journey could have proved commonplace.

Continuing to reason upon these lines I decided that had Davage not been in the habit of carrying duelling pistols around with him, one of them could not have gone off and caused the death of his wife. Or had the lovers taken successful flight before the outraged husband arrived in Lancashire, Lavinia might have lived to have many more portraits painted by Ambrose Keeling and even more borne him the children she never gave to her lawful husband.

Leaving aside the Goodhearts and passing on to the Kermodes: had Gabriel drunk less that New Year's Eve he could have avoided tumbling in the Port St. Mary's harbour and becoming drowned.

Arriving at the present day I considered in turn the case of Bat. *Could* he have avoided violent death by occupying a different position in the race? What if he had been third rider instead of second? Would that have altered his chances of being hurled from his machine into that awkwardly placed telegraph pole?

But enough of supposition!

The Louis Quinz clock on Miss Quinn's mantelpiece chimed the half hour and I took my leave.

A new arrival at the hotel came up and engaged in some quite general conversation which ended us going into the Neptune Bar together. He, too, was new to the island and until dinner we discussed places that he should make a point of seeing. Afterwards he took himself off somewhere: maybe a walk or the cinema and I drifted into the Television Room.

About half past nine one of the staff looked into the darkened room and asked if Mr. Wickham was in there.

'Two visitors for you, sir,' he said, when I had scrambled across feet and between chairs to reach the door. To my delight Vinia was in the hotel lounge with Pale-legs, only of course Gordon Quayle's trousers were rolled down from the knee in the proper position and he wore a pair of sharply pointed leather shoes over his socks.

'I thought you two would like to meet so I persuaded Gordy—'

'Persuaded nothing! Dragooned, don't you mean?' but he smiled agreeably as he said it and I pressed a bell for the waiter.

'You'll have coffee or would you prefer tea? And what sort of drinks?'

Vinia chose a Dubonnet and her nephew Manx beer. Mine was a Scotch. These were brought first, with a tray of tea ordered at the same time. Gordy did not have a great deal to say for himself. In fact Vinia did most of the talking and who was I to quarrel with that? However it seemed polite to bring the boy into our conversation and I asked him to tell me what he did on the Calf. He explained with admirable brevity and seemed amused when I said I had recognised him from a boat trip.

'Oh, I remember now. I was sent down to collect our stuff. Wasn't prepared for how slippery the rocks would be.'

'Seaweed usually is,' Vinia observed, adding that he would do well to buy himself some espadrilles, whereupon we discussed the rival claims of the authentic canvas and rope-soled variety with the newer Italian versions that had been insinuating themselves on to the market. These had a composition sole which did not afford nearly such a good grip and could be positively lethal on damp seaweed.

Vinia nodded and said that when she had been down in Cornwall the previous summer she had seen a man hurt himself quite badly by slipping and coming down flat on his back.

'You know those awful slabby sort of rocks such as you find over at Port Soderic?'

Gordy in turn related how one of the fishermen had told him how a child had slithered off the breakwater into the sea and the man had gone after him to be plagued with a slipped disc ever since and receiving not a word of thanks from the parents of the child.

'Aren't people extraordinary?'

At closer range I could see little resemblance to Lavinia in the boy. It was obvious that he favoured a different set of ancestors. A long time afterwards when I really did see some of the family photographs I was able to trace a much clearer affinity with the Kermode side of the family.

Gordy struck me as a nice lad, immature as yet and certainly dedicated. He saw his time on the Calf as a great opportunity for scientific study of bird life.

'At some future date I hope to be able to go down to the Isles of Scilly, where I'm told they have even more varieties than we can find up here.'

'Isn't there a particular island where birds are kept in a kind of nature preserve?' cut in Vinia.

'Annet, you mean?'

She said that she had very much wanted to go across to the Isles when she was down in Cornwall but it seemed a long trip for very few hours ashore and by helicopter it was too expensive.

'You're a good sailor? But of course you would be.'

'It doesn't follow, Jake. Mother, who's lived by the sea most of her life, can become sick in a rowing boat.'

We smiled with that clubbable air of supremacy which safe sailors cannot quite avoid displaying. *Mal de mer* was all too apt to be regarded as a subject for laughter though to judge by those who have experienced it, it would seem an occasion for the most profound sympathy, where death must be the lesser sting.

Gordy was sleeping ashore that night as the tide was wrong for taking him back to the Calf during the hours of darkness. Even so they left quite early with Vinia's promise to pick me up again in the morning. It was decided to take a packed lunch from each of our hotels and to walk down Glen Helen instead of just driving past it on the way to somewhere else.

The morning was miserable enough for her to 'phone and

suggest we waited a little while to see what improvement might come about later. To eat our sandwiches and fruit in the car under dripping trees did not sound exciting but realising there was not all that amount of time left to us, I suggested waiting until eleven and then chancing things, saying persuasively:

'We could find *something* to do with ourselves, surely?'

'The Manx Museum?' Her tone was mocking.

'There are duller places.'

She relented. 'All right, Jake. I'll be round, rain or shine, and you do some thinking about where to go.'

At five minutes to eleven there was a break in the clouds. By midday we were sauntering down Glen Helen as planned.

3

Nothing in life was more certain than my determination to continue seeing Vinia in London. We had exchanged addresses before parting and my head was full of plans about the future. One day I wanted to take her with me to Cartmel so that she might see the portrait of Lavinia Cushing. Perhaps I wanted to be assured, by watching Sir Justin's own reaction, that the whole thing was not some gigantic confidence trick of mis-memory on my part. Equally I was anxious to meet Vinia's parents and fill in a few gaps in the family story and begin to make the still nebulous figures into people of flesh and blood. Yes I wanted to see what they were like, these Quayles, not least Nat, father of the pleasing youth Gordy.

I think Miss Quinn had been sorry to see me go. As she said any group of islanders formed a pretty close community so that to some, at any rate, the inruption of visitors was welcome. Authors did not flock to 'Ellan Vannin', that 'dear little island' which Caesar was reputed to have called Mona.

'Writers prefer Greece or Capri,' she had said, adding rather tartly that since the Isles of Scilly had received unprecedented publicity owing to Mr. Harold Wilson owning a house there, they would become 'the latest literary menagerie'. Meanwhile the Isle of Man would continue 'to live upon the dimming reputation of Hall Caine.'

'Unless you write a novel about us, Mr. Wickham?' The suggestion was just an open one to take or to discard as I wished.

'I'll give it a thought for the future, Miss Quinn.' On which suitably nebulous promise we said our au revoirs.

I flew back to London Airport and Mrs. T looked as though she were as glad to see me as I was her, for our relationship always had been singularly pleasant and she was totally unlike the dragon-landlady of popular conception.

She asked whether I had enjoyed my visit to the Isle of Man.

'Immensely!'

Such enthusiasm was unfortunate for I am quite sure it gave her the idea that romance had come into my life. This was perfectly true, of course, though I was not ready to admit this fact. Mrs. T doubtless associated seaside resorts as places where young men met attractive girls and vice versa. The trouble was that the majority of so-called romances begun on holiday had a subsequent premature demise. I had experienced this for myself in earlier days when a girl I had thought perfect whilst lazing on the beach of Ilfracombe had seemed all wrong when we met later by arrangement in London. As I recall it today, there had been nothing left to talk about after the first few minutes when we had exhausted the trivia of holiday reminiscence. Fortunately for me she was at heart a pretty sensible girl.

'It's no go, is it Jake?' she had said, after a degree of mutual clock-watching.

'Not really. I'm sorry,' I had added, aware of having bored her as much as she had bored me.

Fiercely, passionately, I was determined this should not happen with Lavinia Quayle.

Work kept me very busy indeed during the coming weeks. The Hall Caine book was finished at last, though my own novel delayed in consequence. However I had had half the advance on Mr. Caine and with formal acceptance of the manuscript more was to come. It was not unlikely that there would be a demand for small alterations—this was usual in such work—but before I became occupied with these it was time to invite Vinia to something. With a certain trepidation I rang the phone number she had given me. A girl with an Australian accent answered. Lavinia had had to go home to see her mother, who was not well.

'Tell her that Jake Wickham phoned, would you?' trying to disguise the ridiculous disappointment with which the news had filled me. Was I right in imagining that Gabrielle Quayle was a bit neurotic since her favourite son's death?

Vinia phoned me the following week, Mrs. T coming to call me with quite a light in the eye which I did my best to disregard. The phone was in the hall; it had one of those sound-proofed hoods round it that one sees in public buildings.

'Jake? It was sweet of you to call me up.'

'I'd have done so before this but I had to rid my system of Hall Caine.'

How was her mother? Nothing serious I hoped?

'She collapsed. The doctor can't find much wrong with her. I suppose it's nerves as much as anything. She's never been the same since Bat—'

'You told me.'

'Did I? Sorry to be such a bore. Anyway I think she was glad to see me.'

Since the surviving son and his wife lived near the parents to expect Vinia to come up from London was a bit much if her mother was not really ill: just perhaps depressed and unhappy.

To change topics I asked who it was that had answered the telephone.

'Oh, Jane, the new girl. She's an Aussy—as no doubt you'll have guessed.'

'It did cross my mind!'

'Was there anything special you wanted, Jake?'

'To see you!'

She paused a minute before asking whether I were quite sure.

'One hundred per cent certain. That satisfy you?'

We made the arrangements to dine together and go on to a show afterwards, leaving two or three choices in case the play-houses were heavily booked. Since Vinia worked in the West End we fixed to meet outside the Criterion Theatre. She looked more formal in her London workaday attire than when wearing holiday clothes but her smile of greeting seemed full of welcome.

'Oh, Jake, it's nice to see you!'

'You're looking very attractive.' The compliment was not original but the best I could manage in my almost tongue-tied confusion. Her glance was as straight as I had remembered but she must have seen I was not merely flannelling.

She seemed taller, but that may have been the town heels. We walked to one of the less chi-chi restaurants near Piccadilly. There was neither bamboo and dim nor chips with everything.

'Bon viveur recommended?' she quipped as we entered.

'Just a Wickham discovery, shall we say?'

Few women know what they wish to order. Either they are avaricious and select the most expensive items on the menu, or else something they may not even particularly like, simply because it happens to be cheap and they have no wish to run their escort into a hefty bill. Vinia had a pleasing mind of her own. She paid me the compliment of assuming that I could afford the place rather than that it would embarrass me if she selected something special. Actually her tastes were sound

118

enough and we did not argue over the wine since we both liked much the same, though she assured me that she would willingly have red if I were sacrificing myself with white because of a slight preference she had expressed.

'The vision of a carafe of one in front of you and the other beside me would spoil the evening, Jake.'

'I can drink either though preferably not on the same occasion!'

There was something about a meal shared which at once made mockery of those 'bachelor messes' unmarried males were supposed to serve to themselves. True I ate out a good deal and was by no means a hopeless cook. All the same—it was then that I found myself thinking of my mother and the times she asked in that serious, mildly concerned way of hers, when I was going to settle down and marry. All at once the idea of unending years with myself at Mrs. T's and Vinia finding new girl after new girl as the others left to get married, seemed a shocking waste: for both of us.

How was I to rate my own standing with this delightful young woman? Had I read too much into her pleasure at seeing me once again? Was it part feminine acting and part good manners? Somehow I did not think so ...

On the island it had been easier. There were places to see, matters to discuss. She was upon home territory and I the visitor to be shown the delights in the best tourist tradition. Here in London we were both on alien ground, for it was no more my real home than it was hers. Just where we both worked and lived our lives.

Vinia seemed relaxed and happy enough as we talked of this and that until it was time to leave for the theatre, just around the corner. She was, I discovered, a serious, absorbed playgoer. To me the theatre was a place for amusement without any great social significance. I had always thought life's problems better dealt with in books, possibly because I myself was an author. As it seemed to me, dramatists created characters which, instead of being able to flower in the minds of the readers had to be projected by the often hit and miss methods of casting.

In an auditorium I rarely became involved with the puppets of the play but Vinia, I could see, was completely carried away into the reality of what we were watching. I had an idea I might have jabbed her with a pin without her noticing.

At the interval she returned to the everyday world with all the reluctance of a deep-sea diver forced to surface when his oxygen tank ran too low for safety.

'Drink?' I suggested.

'If you want one,' putting the onus unfairly on me.

'Not unless you do.'

That did it. She sprang up, full of sweet apology.

'Poor Jake! I should have warned you. I'm always this way in a theatre.'

'It's a bit like a kiddie at her first panto.'

She made a face, saying that I was a hateful man.

The bar was crammed and a harassed woman was running from order to order in attempts to serve everyone before the bells went. My old rugger technique stood me well and I emerged from battle with two glasses only slightly slopped. We drank and discussed the play.

At the end of the evening everyone stood at a kind of attention while a record ground out the Anthem.

'Jake, have you ever thought it's like stopping a movie camera suddenly?' She jerked her head to indicate a man in front of us caught with one arm in and the other out of his coat sleeves.

We decided it did little service to the Queen and might with advantage be dropped except for gala nights and other extra special occasions and whenever royalty were attending in an official capacity.

'Would you like a coffee or something, Vinia?'

'Not for me, we seem to have been eating and drinking quite a lot of the evening.'

'Do you make yourself a hot drink when you get in?'

'Not necessarily. Sometimes on a cold night, maybe, but not in the ordinary way. Why, do you?'

'If I feel like it.'

'I believe really old people on their own make a thermos overnight and have it on the bedtable, in case they wake up.' She shuddered.

'Would you like to end up a lonely old maid?'

'No.'

'I'm glad.'

She looked at me suspiciously, but said nothing.

'Old bachelors aren't all that happy either, I guess.'

But she was not listening. Suddenly she gripped my arm. 'Jake, you know what you said about a sort of fate causing tragedy in certain families? *Hubris* didn't you call it?' I nodded. 'It's funny but now Mother seems to have some such idea in her head. While I was home she tried to read into our family story a kind of malign fate that had been directing things. She believes it is due to a happening way back in the past.'

'*Before* the Cushings you mean?'

'Perhaps. She didn't seem very certain. I don't think she knows much about what went on earlier than grandma Arabella's day. The Kermodes did seem to have pretty rotten luck, didn't they?'

I wondered whether Gabrielle had tumbled unaided to what I still regarded as my own theory. Could I be so sure that Vinia had not talked in such a way as to give a lead?

'Why should Gabrielle—your mother, I mean—suddenly have this idea?'

'It could be something I said, I'm not sure. You see, Jake, I'm beginning to come round to your way of thinking. What troubles me is that if there is anything in the theory—'

'And it *is* only a theory,' I pointed out gently.

She nodded. 'Let us suppose there's a sort of spell on the family. Cast by the Cushings or some malevolent ancestor we don't even know about. How can I be sure that Nat and I won't be affected?' ˙˙

'Have you any reason to think—surely the curse only seems to have struck roughly once in a generation?'

It had claimed Lavinia Cushing and missed her sister Charlotte, the death of whose infant girl and one out of the three sons by violent means I was inclined to discount. New blood kept being brought in on the male side. What befell the early Kermode men was no less than might have been expected in their kind of life. Arabella? Again it might be argued that drunken fishermen were apt to fall into the water if they persisted in walking too close to the edge of the quay.

There was a pattern, yes, but the way it skipped from branch to branch of the family confused things. If *every* female descendant of the Cushing couple suffered personally from the ill luck it might appear—suddenly I knew that I did not want to believe in my own theory any longer because now I, too, had become involved. If the *hubris* idea was correct that meant that Vinia herself might be caught up in the business.

What was it that she had said a moment before?

'How can I be sure that Nat and I won't be affected?'

How indeed ...

4

Two items of minor interest occurred about this time, the first being the announcement of the engagement of a Brendon F. Davage. What connection—if any—was this young man to the Francis Davage who married Lavinia Cushing? Possibly none, though the name was unusual. Still it was not worth pursuing. The bridegroom-to-be was unlikely to feel gratified by being asked whether an ancestor had shot his wife up in Lancashire back in the 19th century!

The other event was an art exhibition of Pre-Raphaelite period paintings to which I had taken myself after hearing the critics lauding it up one Sunday morning.

Art had long been an interest in my life and on Continental trips it was usual to find myself visiting whatever famous gallery there was. In the same way I was often in the Tate or the National Portrait Gallery and rarely missed anything new at the Royal Academy. Time to kill often brought me to the smaller galleries of Mayfair. Probably this instinctive urge to look at a picture, of whatever quality, had ensured that the first thing to attract my attention in Sir Justin's room was bound to have been the Lavinia Cushing portrait.

By right no man should be judged wholly upon the evidence of a single painting and I had accepted Sir Justin's assurance that Ambrose Keeling had no standing in art cricles of his day. Therefore it came as an extraordinarily pleasant surprise to find his name in the catalogue of the exhibition in question. (It was always wise to glance at what was on display before beginning one's round of exploration.)

No. 49. Seascape scene. Ambrose Keeling.

The picture was small-scale, the sort of size which Morland favoured. In subject matter it was pretty poor Turner. There were the creamy sands offset by a grey sea and over the whole, that hint of mist through which the sun might never quite break-clouds. Pretty, evocative, yes. Outstanding? No. Was Keeling then only good at portraiture? Or had that one portrait in particular been his summit of artistic achievement?

The exhibition would be on for another week and it seemed an excuse to 'phone Vinia and tell her. This time she herself answered the telephone, but her reaction was disappointing.

'Oh, Jake! Not an art gallery, please! I'm really not an *affectionada*, you know.'

'Not even when the bait is a picture by Ambrose Keeling? The man who painted Lavinia Cushing?'

She hesitated. If it were another portrait of this 'famous Lavinia of mine' then she might consider going. I really had 'gone off the deep end' as she called it, over his particular picture and thus far succeeded in making her quite anxious to see it. Deflated I admitted that the Keeling on display was but a seascape, honesty making me add that it had no special merit.

'Am I forgiven then, Jake?'

'Of course. It was only an idea.'

'I have a much better one. Why don't you come over and see how the working girls of London live? Might even provide useful copy for one of your books!'

'Authors don't write about their friends as the layman invariably seems to imagine.'

'No? But they dream up lovely stories all about nineteenth century beauties being cruelly done to death by justifiably jealous husbands!' Her laugh was filled with teasing.

'Not that either,' though directly I said this I was sure she did not believe me. Arrangements were made for supper during the week.

'I can't promise which, if any, of the residents will be in, of course,' Vinia stated.

It seemed rude to reply that personally I hoped that the other three would all be out! As it happened they were not.

Vinia had not led me to expect much of the flat. It was in a tall, Victorian Gothic house, up several flights of uncarpeted stone stairs and with those timed electric switches which frequently leave one in darkness half-way between landings. When this happens it is necessary to grope and scratch along the wall for the next switch.

The girls were right at the top: what must originally have been the floor where the servants' bedrooms were. Ceilings became lower and they sloped by the windows as there were gables. The windows themselves were the type referred to as 'dormer'.

The flat had been made gay and colourful by lots of garish scatter cushions; impossibly bright curtains. Lamp shades were kind of Aladdin's hats. All the furniture was in the most off-putting modern designs, however the rocking chair—a narrow

20th century adaptation from the Deep South—proved comfortable.

Vinia had come into what already existed and I could not imagine the decor was entirely to her liking. There was a youthful dash to it which set out to convince the world that emancipation was ever so jolly. I found myself wondering whether the homes of whichever girls founded the community, so to speak, had been unbearably drab. Or did they just like all this colour? Was I being 'square' finding it so unrestful?'

Vinia's flat companions were more interesting than I had expected. There was the Australian, a gaunt young woman, slim as a boy, with weatherbeaten skin and a man's capable hands. She was named Bunty, wore a blouse and denims and worked for an oil company. Dorothy—or Dot-Dot as they occasionally called her—was a model. Very languid, cold and I suspected lazy. She too wore slacks, though these were black velvet and set off by a cossack silk coatee in turquoise which went with her pale hair. The third girl was a cheery tub of a lass, bulging in all the wrong places and untidy. She had splendid chestnut curls—natural, I'll swear—and answered to the nickname of Chips.

The talk was better and more stimulating than anticipated. These young women were well up in world affairs and even the languid Dot-Dot had a brain, though I confess her appearance suggested otherwise. Or perhaps it was part of the necessary character-study?

I do not know who prepared the meal; whether it was a communal effort or not, but it was nicely set out on unmatching china which they informed me had come from job-lots.

'We're pretty heavy on breakages,' and Vinia smiled. 'I've picked one of the better kind for you, Jake.'

They had made prawn cocktails after which came a shaghetti dish served in a pot of curiously familiar shape. Chips burst out laughing at my ill-disguised astonishment.

'It *was*, but it's been scoured and boiled and what-have-you. Latest thing in Italy, I swear.'

I spluttered over my wine (a Spanish red cruder than I liked.)

'She brought it back with her,' Dot-Dot interpolated. 'It's not from Portobello, where most of our treasures are acquired.'

They had a cold sweet to follow, some kind of trifle affair dreamed-up, no doubt, in a woman's magazine. Vinia, knowing my preference for cheese, produced a Danish blue and cheddar. The coffee was Maxwell House but they had cream to go with it and a liqueur which the Australian had brought back from the Continent. (One of those 'cycling across Europe' affairs.)

The fact that I was an author seemed to interest them and to my surprise Chips had read Hall Caine's *The Deemster*.

'Found it lying around at home. My papa is a terrible collector of books and I suppose he picked it up at some time.'

'You and Chips can have a heart-to-heart about Mr. Caine while we three clear and wash-up.'

I insisted upon doing my share of the chores and must confess to never having had a merrier session at the sink. A novice to procedure at bachelor girl parties I was not sure whether the rest of the evening would be spent in the same way or not. However Dot-Dot took herself off to her own room and the none-too-muted sounds of Pop music, whilst Bunty had a lengthy telephone conversation in the hall. Since the house was in the S.T.D. network, I wondered how the bills might be fairly shared.

'Are you two dying to be left alone?' Chips asked with her impudent little grin. Vinia looked mildly annoyed: the first time that I had seen her put out.

'For heaven's sake!' she exclaimed.

It seemed left to me to arbitrate and what could I do but say, 'Of course not!' Still the dear girl did use a long time finding her knitting in her own room. This enabled me to take Vinia up on the matter of her momentary displeasure.

'You didn't seem to like the implication Chips made just now, Vinia.'

'Forget it!'

'You must know that pleasant though I find your three friends, *you* are the one I came to see.'

She looked suddenly serious. 'Jake, aren't you letting things rush along rather? We've not known each other long and already I feel as though you—you expect something to come of our friendship.'

'Would that be so surprising?'

'You've filled your head with a lot of romantic stories about my ancestors. Tried to see in me a likeness to Lavinia Cushing and because of that seem to imagine yourself falling in love with me.'

'I don't have to imagine anything because it happens to be true.'

This shook her greatly. All the poor girl could do was to keep saying how absurd it was. What did I really know about her?

'All that I need to know,' by which time I was kneeling, (foolishly no doubt) beside her chair, reaching for one of the nervously fidgetting hands and telling her that I had fallen in love with her and no one else. How it had happened for the first time in my life, anything which had taken place in the past being completely irrelevant.

'It's sweet of you to say all this, Jake. Don't think I fail to appreciate—'

There was something about her manner which made me aware that all was not well.

'You know very little about me, my dear,' she went on, speaking almost as a mother might to her child. Absurd that in seconds she should be imagining herself older: more wordly wise than myself.

Doubtless my tone was stubborn. 'One doesn't have to have reasons for loving someone.'

'That's true I suppose.'

'I realise it's probably much too soon, but I wanted you to know my feelings.'

'Yes. Thank you for that, Jake.' Still the rather sad remote air persisted. It should have warned me that Vinia might be involved already in a love affair with someone else. Stupidly, obstinately even, I had never stopped to think that that might be the case. She left the chair abruptly and went across to the apology for a window, standing with her back to me, saying she wished that I had not brought up the subject.

'I'm not going to pretend that I wasn't aware that you rather liked me, Jake. I kept telling myself that really all it was was probably a sort of hangover of your strange obsession with the first Lavinia's portrait. Whether a person really can fall in love with a painting, I can't say. I enjoyed your company over in the island and there seemed nothing against meeting again. As a matter of fact I haven't that number of friends in London.'

This was a long speech by her standards and my suspicion deepened that there was something she could not quite bring herself to tell me. She was, as it were, feeling her way and any minute now Chips was liable to rejoin us: the reason, perhaps, why we both appeared a little tense.

'Jake, you've taken it for granted that I'm not involved with anyone. Perhaps it was wrong of me to allow this false impression to grow. If I were actually engaged, I'd probably have been wearing a ring. Then you could have told right away.'

It could be said that not all couples made a ring first 'must' when it came to betrothal. There were those who preferred to divert the expense into some other article or who were too hard up to buy a decent ring at the time so preferred to wait.

'Does this mean that you're committed—if that's the right word?'

She bent her head and answered 'Yes' in a low, unhappy voice. Then: 'It's a long story, Jake, and we're not likely to be alone more than another minute or so. Bunty's hung up the receiver and Chips must have found her knitting by now. They're only being tactful.'

'You would prefer to discuss it some other time?'

'Please, it isn't easy to explain—in two or three minutes. The fact is I'm not entirely a free agent.'

'I understand. I won't talk about it again.'

She turned, warm and generous, her hands outstretched to me and tears in her eyes. 'It's great—*knowing* how you feel, Jake.'

If Chips did open the door at that moment, I am afraid that neither of us heard her.

Any author's daily post varies considerably in contents. One day it will be all official looking but on another there may be abusive or appreciative fan mail to be answered since ignoring such communications—unless anonymous—suggests deplorable manners. Never having seen Vinia's writing hitherto I was not to recognise the envelope. She stated in her simple forthright fashion that it would be easier to explain things in a letter than to tell me direct.

For you see, Jake dear, I do happen to like you quite a lot.

To be honest, this had suggested itself in those few moments before Chips rejoined us.

Things do not always work out in life exactly as one might wish and there may be commitments, made for what seemed to be most valid of reasons at the time, which are exceedingly difficult to ignore.

It would be superfluous and much too personal to quote her letter to me verbatim, but the main facts were as follows: with just a few of her comments to go with them.

Whilst the Quayles were still living in the Isle of Man—this was somewhat before Bat's death in the motor cycle contest—there was a friend of the two boys and, for that matter, the family as a whole, who was greatly attracted to Lavinia. He was a Manxman called Rod Kneen—what an odd way they spelt the surname over there!—well off by local standards:

We went around together as a foursome quite a lot. That is, my brothers Rod and myself. It seemed generally accepted that Rod and I would end up engaged.

Nothing so far had altered the general trend. She wrote of liking this man: being fond of him, even, and how he was very much bound up with the happy relationship between herself and her brothers. The fact that the dead twin had liked Rod may have counted with her for something, too. However this alone did not amount to a situation of inordinate difficulty. What followed, however, complicated matters.

Rod was the son of an advocate. Members of the Bench and Bar required special training in Manx law and in brief the set-up was this. The High Court of Justice had three divisions. Serious crime was dealt with by the Court of General Gaol Delivery presided over by Mr. Hall Caine's Deemster (which meant a 'giver of dooms' or judgements). Less serious offences came before the High Bailiff, the equivalent of our stipendiary magistrates and Justices of the Peace. Barristers and solicitors were combined into the single office of Advocate, much as upon the Continent.

After Bat's death when Gabrielle began to go to pieces in the running of her guest house, family finances grew critical. The Quayles had to borrow money. The loan limit chargeable on the island (dating back to the law of 1691 and reaffirmed in 1921) was six per cent. Pawnshops and Bills of Sale were alike illegal, so no help there. In short the Quayle financial affairs in some way came up against Manx Law—Vinia did not explain how and may well not have known.

If it hadn't been for the help given us by Rod and his father —Rod was himself then studying law—*my parents might have been in very great difficulties indeed. As it was things were only just about put right on their behalf.*

Therefore it seemed there had been every reason to leave the island. On Vinia's authority neither Gabrielle nor her husband had been back there. It must have been around this time that Nat had married and settled permanently on the mainland.

Rod still lives in Castletown. In fact it was his car that I borrowed over there.

130

That shook me, so convinced was I by its colour that it belonged to some girl. Evidently visiting her nephew, Gordy, had not been her sole purpose in returning to the island, as the last page of her letter proved. Rod was becoming tired of waiting for her to make up her mind about marrying. Doubtless he was justified in pointing out that they had known one another long enough. (I trusted that he would be too much of a gentleman to recall services rendered to her family.)

I pleaded for time, Jake. This was all before I met you, I should mention.

Rod did not try to press her further at that stage. He was busy and she had the excuse of wishing to see how Gordy was faring on the Calf of Man.

Rod simply said, 'Here's the car,' and I gratefully accepted. When I had met you I phoned to say there was an acquaintance of Blanche Quinn's whom I had promised to show around as he was writing a book about the island.

I suppose that Rod had seen her off: certainly I had not dared to offer at that stage of our acquaintance.

So there's the situation, Jake. I am supposed to be reflecting on the matter, here in London...He has already written twice to know my answer.

Vinia was in a definite quandary. On the one hand was this young advocate to whom she had a considerable indebtedness and, one assumed, knew with the thoroughness of long acquaintance. And on the other side—myself, the man for whom she seemed to feel a genuine attraction.

5

No doubt it had been foolish, assuming her to be free. Even more ridiculous to seek some parallel between this and the Lavinia Davage situation, with myself as Keeling to complete the triangle. Vinia was not married—yet and surely there was bound to be a victory for common sense. I did not know what sort of a character Kneen was but it was inconceivable that he would force a girl to marry him. Indeed why should any sensible man wish such a thing: much less expect a union to succeed when all the love was upon one side.

Vinia's reluctance to hurt him I could condone: understand, too, her feelings of gratitude for whatever the legal services were that father and son had provided for her family. I suspected her of being loyal and stubborn—with that chin!

Well finally, of course, she must decide between us. If, as I so hoped her fondness for me was indeed love, then she must not allow herself to settle for second best with Rod Kneen. There were no steps I would not be prepared to take, once I knew for sure that I had gained her love.

Meanwhile the situation was delicate, to say the least.

I acknowledged her letter, thanking her for having stated things as frankly and asking when we could meet for discussion. She was welcome to visit my digs where there might be greater privacy than the flat. Indeed Mrs. T had been known to allow the use of her own sitting room for privileged lodgers amongst whom I dared count myself. The Author's Club to which I belonged did not allow ladies on the premises. This left the National Book League which might be pleasantly empty or very full. Here, too, the most private of the public rooms was exclusive to members.

Vinia rang me to say that whilst she agreed we would have 'to talk things over' sometime, just then she was very caught up as her brother Nat was down in London to attend some meeting to do with the motor industry's agents.

'Am I right in thinking you'd like to meet him, Jake?' Her voice was mischievous.

Would I!

'Acting on that assumption I did a bit of sales talk about you and he'll be free to dine with us tomorrow, if that isn't too short notice?'

There was an executive of a literary society up on whose council I was but this would be over by six at the latest. Even if it were not, I intended to leave by then, and since Nat was staying at the Regent Palace this seemed a sensible place to meet. Skipping out of committee proved less easy than I had hoped and it was six thirty when I took a taxi through the thick of London's rush hour traffic. Luck—and at least some of the lights—were with us. I hurried in to the hotel to find Vinia and her brother already having a sherry.

He was a nice looking man, recognisable as Gordy's father and with a fine, firm handclasp. The blue eyes were the same as Lavinia's and so was the shape of his nose.

'I can't pretend to have read any of your books,' he admitted cheerfully, having ascertained my drink requirement.

'At least that's honest. Nothing is more embarrassing to a writer than the person who pretends to have read one of one's novels and is hoping to Heaven not to be questioned as to which!'

'Afraid I read thrillers and travel stories.'

'Jake doesn't turn out light romance, Nat! They're straight fiction.'

He grinned, saying he liked his just a shade crooked. We talked about what had brought him to London and Vinia's flat, which he had seen for the first time minus two of its regular residents. As 'the palace' was filling up it seemed advisable to go into dinner. When we were settled he turned to me.

'I understand that you're writing about the island, Wickham.'

I explained that the Hall Caine book was completed. 'There was a lot besides to interest me over there.'

'So my sister was telling me. What is it exactly that you want to know?'

'Suppose you tell me a little about the war years in Castletown for a start?'

This he did well and interestingly. Whilst life had been less difficult than in beleagured Britain, the war by no means left them undisturbed. Even in a relatively safe area, there was always the sea and danger from enemy shipping.

'It was worst around the area covered by the Ramsey life boat. I remember the excitement in—let me see, it must have been nineteen forty-one I suppose, when an Aberdeen trawler called *The Strathairlie* was stranded in the surf. The coxswain took the boat alongside thirteen times. They were damned nearly wrecked themselves. Gave the chap a medal for his courageous work.'

Nat spoke of his schooling in which, of course, I was extremely interested. This surprised him.

'Didn't know you'd been in the teaching profession yourself.' Nat turned to his sister as though the omission was hers. To be truthful I am not sure that at the time she knew.

One gathered that the mother, Gabrielle, had managed—as women did—in wartime, finding enough food for her growing twin sons and the baby that was to become the Lavinia of today. Food was easier, presumably, in rural districts than in the cities. As wife Gabrielle must have carried the secret burden of worry over her husband, whenever he was away on active service which, except for short leaves, would have been the greater part of those years. The impression of her was of someone quiet and loving. Neither Nat nor Vinia said anything which gave a real clue to the personality of their mother. They were much better about Martin Quayle.

'When Dad come home on leave we had a high old time, I can tell you. Vinia was too small to remember.'

This she denied with vigour, claiming to recall the shock to her infant susceptibilities when he appeared with an ugly red-brown beard.

'Oh, how it tickled!'

Nat laughed saying that had been when their father had been on the Archangel run.

'Too damned cold to shave in those parts, my girl.'

She conceded this with her usual grace.

'Things changed when Dad lost his arm. He had a grudge against Hitler and all his henchmen: the world in general.' The speaker frowned. 'Because he wasn't in till the end, I guess.'

'Surely he would have recognised the limitations it would impose in his peacetime occupation as well?'

Nat nodded. Trawlermen with one arm could be a liability.

'That's why he switched to the guest house idea, once peace came and brought the visitors back to the island.'

'But took you and your twin away from it?'

'That was inevitable, surely? We'd never looked on ourselves as island people in the way Dad and Mum were, who had been born there. And you, too, Vinia, who saw first light in Castletown.'

The young men had sought the opportunities of the mainland, as Nat explained. By the end of hostilities the island had everything to work up to achieve something approaching its pre-war popularity. All the internees had to be dispersed. Places de-requisitioned: money till then needed for more important things diverted into rehabilitation as a pleasure centre for tourists.

'Take the lifeboat service, which I suppose I know a bit about, since my father used to help in it. At the end of the war Douglas needed a new boat—and had it, thanks to the Manchester and Salford life-boat Fund. Port Erin's was six years old in '46. Port St. Mary's was serviceable for just another two years and Ramsey's lasted to the same date then that also needed replacing.'

'At least the Isle of Man must have been luckier than the

135

Isle of Wight,' and I recounted some of the damage from enemy action which they had sustained.

'On the whole we were lucky, as communities went,' he agreed. 'I suppose Bat and I could have remained to help, but we wanted jobs with a future.'

'Perfectly natural.'

'The parents soldiered on while Vinia went to school.'

'And you married.'

'True. I hope you'll meet my wife one of these days. She's the tops.'

'You've certainly produced an extraordinarily nice son between you.'

'So glad you liked Gordy. Then most people do.' He was not being boastful in saying this, though Vinia went through the motions of blowing a trumpet. In all this time Bat had been mentioned only once. Being keenly interested in what sort of relationship existed between fraternal twins (whether they were as close—though not as alike, as the identical variety) I was wondering how tactfully to introduce the topic when Nat did so himself.

'Would you say we were all that alike, Vinia? There was a similarity in looks, I suppose, but it was not bad enough for us to be confused. Undoubtedly we had a bond ... A kind of intuition which would tell me if Bat were ill or worried about something, no matter what the distance between us. I won't say we had all the same illnesses. In childhood measles, maybe; then a lot of the other boys had it as well and I'd say it was proximity as much as anything. Our tastes were surprisingly different. I sort of have the family love of messing about in boats. Living in the Midlands that is a thing I greatly miss. But Bat couldn't care less about boats. For him it was machinery.'

'Didn't he join the same firm as yourself?'

'That wasn't the reason. He was a taker-to-pieces and builder-upper! Clocks! Watches! He loved nothing better than having them in bits and putting everything back to make it work better than before. Speed!' Nat smiled wryly. 'The only boat he cared a tinker's cuss for was to go out in the *Nancy Belle* speed boat in Douglas Bay. As a nipper he would race on his push bike, crouched over the handlebars as if he were entering that Paris Grand Prix—if that's what it's called.'

I was conscious of Vinia beside me, twisting and twisting her handkerchief around her fingers, determined not to disgrace us both by tears.

'Bat was a grand, intuitive sort of person. He could take short cuts to gain results where I have to plod along the orthodox way.' Very quietly Nat added that he had worshipped his brother and said so in such a way that it did not sound slop.

This was too much for poor Vinia who with a muffled excuse left us and was away, one assumed in the powder room, for quite a while and when she came back, rather bright eyed but calm, we had stopped talking about Bat.

In the interval though Nat explained his own sense of loss and bewilderment over his brother's death and the disintegration of his mother's personality.

'She's never got over it to this day. I can only describe her as an entirely different person. Shut in upon herself, if you can understand. Dad does his best for her.' Nat sighed. 'There isn't much laughter left in them and when we were nippers there used to be so much.'

The possibility that Psychiatric treatment might have helped crossed my mind and with it a slight unease lest this tendency to melancholia be inherited. Sorrow might have unhinged Arabella Kermode and been handed on to her daughter when in turn a cruel accident took away a deeply loved member of the family. Gabrielle's childhood may not have been all that happy: losing her mother and then being adopted. Or was I reading altogether too much into the story from the past? Was it not enough to unhinge—ever so slightly—any mother who was a bystander when her son's head struck the telegraph pole as he was hurled from his motor cycle?

'Bat was everyone's favourite. The bright boy. The boy with the taking ways.'

E*

Nat's words were in my ears, even as I watched Lavinia walking back towards our table.

Could the twins' popularity have been one reason for Nat's early marriage, habit though this had become amongst the post-war young? He would have found himself through being loved because he was Nat—and not just the brother of his better-liked twin. I meant to discuss this theory sometime with Lavinia and seek her views. Much as I wanted her with us I would not greatly have minded if her absence had lasted five further minutes during which time I might have had a chance to ask her brother about Rod Kneen. Now the opportunity was lost—perhaps for ever.

There was no need for her to apologise; her tentative smile, first to him then to me, did this for her.

Shortly after ten Vinia said she should be going and Nat came to the tube station with us. She became very modern-independent at my offer to see her home, saying it was quite ridiculous to go right out of my way. In the end we watched her disappear down on the escalator after she had kissed her brother good-bye by the ticket machines and given me a handwave.

Nat turned. 'Care for a drink?'

This seemed an idea and he evidently had the popular impression that authors liked late hours. We repaired to an inn which was reached via one of the exits from the station.

Nat said that he gathered I was 'smitten' with his sister. I agreed, though considered ' "smitten" rather an inadequate expression to my feelings.'

He nodded.

'I suppose I shouldn't ask this, but did she indicate at all—'

'Why else should the poor girl be worried about Rod Kneen? You know about him?'

'I rather hope you might tell me more about him.'

Nat said that he knew Rod but only slightly—nowadays Kneen was well off and ran a yacht. One gathered the friendship with Vinia had developed more strongly after the twins left the island. Kneen senior was a person of considerable standing.

'Between them they saved our folks from quite a packet of trouble to do with the guest house. Debts, one thing and another. Young Rod seems to have run away with the idea that this gives him a special claim upon Vinia. Frankly I don't see it—and told her so.'

My heart warmed to Nat.

'You know what women are, Wickham. In my sister's case loyal to the point of stupidity. Until you came along I guess she was all set to accept him.'

'Surely he can't take her agreement for granted? It isn't as if there were any official engagement between them.'

'Ah! But morally speaking, "understandings" can be almost as binding.' He smiled as he said this. 'And you don't quite know Vinia yet. Also I suspect that you idealize her. Remember she is stubborn. We Quayles are—with the possible exception of poor old Bat. She'll need to be convinced more of your happiness than her own.'

'How—'

He shrugged, then: 'May I suggest, Wickham—hadn't I better start calling you Jake?'

'Please do.'

'Jake, then ... suggest that for the present you try playing things by ear. Vinia will go over all the arguments in her own mind. She always does. On the one hand there'll be what she thinks of as her duty. Against this must be weighed the degree of her love for you. Frankly at this stage I don't think we can judge either the depth or the strength of this. Take heart, though. She's a sensible lass. I think it would be the greatest mistake to seek to force her to choose between the pair of you.'

With that I was in entire agreement.

'Mind you she won't want to upset Rod. He's had his uses in our lives. He's a decent, honourable chap—so far as I know and I cannot really believe he would want an unwilling bride.

Materially he can offer quite a lot. Then so, I imagine, can you.'

My gesture was half satirical as I answered:

'Enough, perhaps.'

'But no yacht?' He grinned and in that moment contrived to look the same age as his son, making me forget that Nat was in fact thirty-six.

'Does Vinia like sailing?'

'I'll say she does! For Dad it was trawlers. For me, ships in general but for my kid sister definitely yachts.'

Rather facetiously I said that if I managed to sell the American paper back rights of some of my books I might be able to afford a very modest boat:

'A second hand Catamaran or a chuck-out from some regatta.'

Nat said that Rod Kneen's yacht was not all that magnificent. 'Hardly the sort of thing that that tea chap, Sir Thomas Lipton, wasn't it? used to own before the war. I've seen pictures of his *Shamrock*, as I believe it was called.' Nat kissed the tip of his fingers reminiscently.

The preparations of closing up the bar had begun and the waiters swallowed yawns, doubtless blessing the English licencing laws which meant customers being thrown out at 11 p.m.

We rose and walked back towards Nat's hotel.

'It's been nice meeting you, Jake. I hope to see you up our way sometime.' With that he held out his strong-gripping hand. Having said good-bye I caught a No. 59 'bus which would take me most of the way home.

6

To walk slap into Blanche Quinn in Museum Street was unexpected to say the least, though it has been stated that sooner or later one encounters 'the world and his wife' in our great city. However the explanation was simple. She had come over to do some work in the British Museum Reading Room—whither I myself was bent. Miss Quinn had done what she called 'a preliminary foray' and filled in slips for the books to be ready for the morning: an economy in time practised by most who used the library frequently.

'I'm staying with my sister out at Beaconsfield, Mr. Wickham.'

Abandoning the intention to proceed on to the Museum I asked if I might give her coffee somewhere. The choice was not great in that area but we selected what looked to be the least *avant garde* of the places. One wondered how that famous old Bloomsbury set of the Virginia Wolf period would have liked all those gooey cakes and hissing espresso machines!

Anxious to return some of the hospitality afforded me by Miss Quinn over on the island I suggested that she might care to dine with me and do a show. She seemed delighted.

'Do you know I've not seen *The Mousetrap*?'

That I had, fortunately long enough ago to have forgotten it, did not matter. We made a tentative date and she left me her address, then apologised for having another appointment. On the pavement outside the café she asked whether I had seen anything of Lavinia Quayle and on being answered in the affirmative, smiled.

'I imagined that you might have done! Well, au revoir,' and she walked off into the opposite direction from mine.

The theatre tickets were procured and there were several reasonably good restaurants in the vicinity. Miss Quinn was punctual, which one expected of her. When we had settled what to eat I mentioned Nat's visit to London.

'How did you like him?'

'Very much.' Somehow I had to bring conversation round to the subject of Rod Kneen. She would probably know his father anyway.

'Rodney Kneen the advocate's son? He runs quite a showy

little yacht. Don't ask me in what class, since I don't know the first thing about boats! He takes part in most of the island regattas. Now I come to think of it, I believe the craft is named the *Lavinia*.'

That had to be!

'They are fairly close friends.' I was feeling for my words, not wishing to betray any confidences. At the same time I was anxious to learn more about my rival.

'Friends? Obviously, since he called his boat after her!' Miss Quinn smiled, then fell to studying her wine glass with a myopic, concentrated stare. 'I have met Rodney's father once or twice. A quiet, desiccated man, with a brilliant legal mind. I gather that Rodney himself is rather different. More—shall we call it showy? Very interested in all local activities, even down to the sheep dog trials!'

Showy? Perhaps that explained the pale blue car, an affectation of colour-choice more understandable from an undergraduate than a man in his late-twenties or early thirties. (I did not know his age.)

'So you think there may be an attachment between this young man and Miss Quayle? Then I must be mistaken.'

I was puzzled. 'Mistaken—how?'

'Well it had occurred to me that Miss Quayle seemed quite interested in yourself.'

'She is—I mean—we—. Oh, lord I'm making a frightful mess of this, aren't I?'

The logical lady suggested that it might be simpler if I were to start 'at square one'. She heard me out attentively before giving her opinion which was that if Vinia were really in love with me, she must refuse Rodney Kneen. On the other hand if she were genuinely uncertain as to which of us she preferred, as a woman, 'she would play for time'. Miss Quinn suggested that since the two young people were friends of long standing it ought to be possible for Lavinia to approach him in perfect frankness. 'You are still doubtful, Mr. Wickham?'

I explained that Vinia felt indebted to him in respect of the help which he and his father had given the Quayles at a time of financial difficulty.

'In the old days a daughter might sacrifice herself in such a way, Mr. Wickham, but not in the nineteen sixties!' with which mild rebuff Miss Quinn changed the subject.

She enjoyed the play greatly. Then Miss Quinn was by no means unique, as an intellectual, in liking thrillers of the Christie school. They were relaxing and at the same time their problems could hold the interest of the mind until the *denouément*. We parted in good spirits, making a tentative arrangement to meet again whilst she was over here.

I was determined to see Vinia on her own and had written so. She telephoned to say that she would be away for the weekend with her parents who liked frequent visits from their daughter. She 'could not prevent my coming, if such was my wish.' The local hotel was called "the Artichoke." Really it's just a small commercial but clean and not bad, I fancy.'

'Are you inviting me then?'

'It would be company on the journey. Though mind you, we wouldn't see all that much of each other when we were there. I daresay you could look up Nat and, from what I know of you, you're dying to meet my parents.'

'Since I have every hope that we shall be much closer to one another in the future—'

My boldness went unrewarded. 'If you're going to be tiresome, the offer's withdrawn, Jake.'

The journey up to Stretton-le-Soke was pleasant in a way that an ordinary trip from London to the Midlands would not have been. By her stipulation intimate topics were taboo, but the companionship enjoyed over on the island was simple to re-establish. There was enough in the daily news for discussion and mild argument. We lunched in the dining car mostly to break up the travelling time and because the buffet meant standing up to a small counter or swaying, cup or glass in hand with nothing more interesting to eat than those cellophane-shielded sandwiches and snippets of slab cake or else pies and wafer-lined biscuits, chocolate coated.

'What's Stretton-le-Soke like, Vinia? I've never been there.'

She smiled. 'Neat council estates. Factories. A bit of river tucked away to the north and quite a grand municipal park complete with floral clock. The town has what you'd expect. Colossal branch of the Co-Op. Gas and electric showrooms offering everything that is latest on "attractive h.p. terms". Chain stores. Betting shops. And cycling ones, too—for workers still like a bike—in Stretton. The cinemas have gone over to bingo or ten pin bowling and there isn't any theatre.'

'Sounds 'orrible!'

'It is rather. One can understand why the youth of the place finds life so boring.'

The housing estates had their own shops which Vinia said 'charged accordingly' there being no direct competition. Few women inclined to push prams and trolley shopping baskets to the main thoroughfare.

'Nat is rooted there by his job. One could say he and Grace have as good a life in Stretton as anywhere else. But Gordy won't stay. Of that I'm sure. Probably end up at some wildfowl trust or—isn't it Skomer, in South Wales, where they have a bird sanctuary?'

All this sounded more like a hobby than a career, though I had to admit to ignorance as to the ways in which a young man interested in ornithology and marine studies might earn his living.

When we reached Stretton I found it hard to understand why Nat should have chosen this in preference to remaining on the Isle of Man. However purely from the commercial angle, Stretton won: the great sprawling acreage of car works was enough to give the town its prosperity. Outside in the 'executive's residential area' there would be splendidly equipped houses and expensively dressed occupants with two cars instead of just one. Holidays abroad would stretch beyond the confines of Europe's conventional playgrounds and the

144

sons and daughters were more than likely to win places to University. Such was the remarkable development in a society which had turned almost a complete circle since the Industrial Revolution.

'The Artichoke' hotel was as hundreds up and down the country: part garishly modern: part dingily old-fashioned. For all the flash cocktail bar with its black leather-seated chairs and sofas, there were still the labyrinthian passageways upstairs linking landings with but one bathroom between half a dozen or so rooms. Though there was re-lay radio on the wall by the bed, the furniture was huge and ugly.

Having said au revoir to Lavinia I was accountably depressed and an after-dinner stroll round the town did little to dispel this feeling. Youths and girls hung around in groups or huddled in doorways. Instead of feeling abusive towards them one felt sympathetic. Before long most of them would be heading for London ...

Nat had invited me over to lunch next day and except that all the houses on the estate seemed erected at odd angles—to catch the sun or to avoid the worst of the wind——the impression was less of jerry-building than some seen in the south. The rooms were not big but everything was conveniently planned from the sliding doors which divided up the living rooms to the cupboard space and working surfaces in the photogenic-looking kitchen. His wife was a plain girl with a cheerful disposition. Her voice and regional accent were flat to my critical ears but she was likeable in the extreme. All her movements were quick and bustling. She served an excellently cooked meal: better than the previous night's dinner at 'The Artichoke', an hotel they both described as 'not much cop'.

'We'd have put you in Gordy's room if Vinia only had told me.'

'Really I'm perfectly comfortable.'

Grace Quayle made a face at me. 'You Southerners are so damned polite!'

'Actually I'm from the North,' and I laughed at her surprise.

145

They were justifiably proud of their little home and Grace had showed me the two upstairs bedrooms and 'usual offices' which she and Nat had decorated between them. Gordy's room had various bird photos and exhibits which his mother said she dared not touch.

'You'd have been more comfortable here, I'm sure, Mr. Wickham.'

During the afternoon they took me for a run round the district in the mini-car which Nat was able to buy at special discount through the firm. Whatever one might think of the Midlands as a whole, the countryside was much more easily accessible than in London where an hour or longer would be needed to reach the so-called Green Belt. Within ten minutes of the Municipal clock-tower in Stretton-le-Soke's Derby Road, we were in arable country with good views on the hillier sections. I gave them tea out and returned with them for a cold snack, during which Vinia turned up looking rather tired. Since she had not seen her sister-in-law for some time the two girls gossiped out in the kitchen under guise of washing-up whilst we watched television.

Vinia returned to outline the morrow's plans. Nat and Grace were visiting some people called Harris but expected to drop in at the senior Quayles for morning coffee on the way. It appeared that I was expected there for tea and Vinia insisted upon the necessity to call for me.

'Surely you don't think I'll become lost?'

'You don't know how confusing blocks of council flats can be, when you haven't an idea how the numbers run.'

Nat grinned in my direction but held his peace.

Sunday morning being blank I decided to visit the extremely modern church, in appearance not unlike the concrete circular vents to deep shelters in South London. The padre was young and enthusiastic: the congregation more sizeable than might have been expected. And after church, the Malt Shovel offered a change from the hotel.

'Mother's very *triste* at the moment,' Vinia announced, when she collected me. 'It's near Bat's birthday, which always makes her worse.'

'It is also Nat's birthday—'

'I know, Jake, but she—doesn't see it as logically as that.'

The estate was not quite so complicated as Vinia maintained, though difficult enough, with tier upon tier of brightly painted balconies and front doors which had a number system that only the originator can have mastered. Notices such as '2 Block, 1—45' did little to lessen confusion.

'You *see*!'

'Given time, I should have found the right flat.'

Gabrielle opened and I was shocked by her appearance. She looked ill, with the bleached skin of a woman who went out too seldom. Her hair was almost white. At one time she must have been tall and well-set-up: now she was bent and stooping like an old lady. The eyes were dull but in the half light I guessed they were the same colour as her daughter's.

'Welcome, Mr. Wickham,' Gabrielle said, in a quietly modulated voice. (Nothing about her could have been strident.) She wore a drab grey two-piece which another woman would doubtless recognise as a chain-store purchase.

Martin was a strapping fellow still, his hair grizzled, but otherwise he was younger-looking than his wife. In his face, too, lines of care were grooved about nose and mouth. To my surprise he had no artificial arm: just an empty-sleeve tucked into his jacket pocket. From what one could tell, the arm had been amputated at shoulder-level which may have presented a more difficult problem.

'My daughter tells me that you've fallen in love with our island,' Martin exclaimed.

I would not have put my feelings quite so strongly as that! However it made a useful conversational opening. While the womenfolk were seeing to tea he told me several interesting new facts about Man.

'Have you seen "the courting chairs" over Ballafreer way? In a farm garden. Actually they're a couple of inter-twining

147

yews which form the seats. They were mentioned as being old well over a hundred years ago. There's also a peculiar rock known as the white lady of Ballafreer.'

'Any special reason?'

'Well, it's white quartz. Stands seven foot high. They say it brings fortune to young brides.'

'Did Mrs. Quayle try her luck with it?'

He shook his head. 'Maybe it would have been better for us if she had.'

Martin was disappointed that I had not attended the famous outdoor service at Kirk Braddan.

'Let me see now. I think it started in eighteen fifty six because the church itself only held two hundred souls. More had to be turned out, so the vicar took the service in the churchyard instead. And I bet you didn't discover anything about our rather dubious celebrity, Capt. Hugh Crow.'

'The slave trader? But I did and gather that on the whole he was humane.'

'The blacks—I forget, the *non-whites*'—carefully he made the amendment, 'were called Jim Crows after him.'

Gabrielle had been baking and, to one who perforce has to make do with bought cakes, this was a pleasant surprise. She became more animated once she could be drawn out to talk. It struck me that she may also have been shy. There was so much I longed to ask: about Arabella, her mother, about her childhood and all that had happened in or around Port St. Mary, but it was evident conversation was being kept off island matters. Vinia's several warning glances made me realise this fact. However she could not prevent my noticing the photograph on top of the T.V. set, or wandering across to look at it. It could only be Bat. He was not, in truth, all that like his brother. It was an eager, questing face and one could understand a mother's anguish at losing such a boy.

'I see you are looking at my son, Bartholomew,' Gabrielle said.

(Had they really called him by his full name?)

'Yes. I've heard a lot about him.'

'He was a fine rider,' cut in Martin. 'That is why we shall never understand how he came to grief in the race.'

'It was the Smith boy's fault, Martin, and you know it.'

'I never questioned the fact, my dear.'

Gabrielle turned to me, pleadingly. 'Wouldn't you agree, Mr. Wickham, that the course should be re-routed?'

I had to confess ignorance of the finer points in motor cycle racing and what were the possibilities of altering a course acceptable over so many years.

'We tried to get up a petition—' her voice faded.

'My dear, we were warned of the hopelessness of our task by the Kneens. Unfortunately there have been other accidents, though not always at the same spot. If that had been a fact, then there might have been a stronger argument.'

'The T.T. Races and the Manx Grand Prix bring too much trade to the island for them to be shown up for what they are. An invitation to suicide.'

'Mother, that is a great exaggeration.' Vinia spoke soothingly, as she might have done to a fractious child. 'There is an element of risk in any form of sport. Boxing—steeple-chasing —Brand's Hatch—'

'Surely ping pong's pretty safe?' by which absurdity I hoped —and indeed succeeded—in bringing conversation back to a lighter vein.

When it was time for me to leave Martin said that he could do with a stroll and would walk with me to 'The Artichoke'.

'I'm sorry you brought up the subject of Bat, Wickham.'

'Yes. I realise it was tactless of me.'

'Up till then you could say we were a happy family. Even this—' he indicated his infirmity, 'was not much to lose considering what some fellows suffered. At most it has been— inconvenient. But when Bat was killed every darned thing began to go wrong for us. My wife lost heart in running the guest house. Debts piled up. We were in a pretty state, I can tell you. That's why we're always so beholden to the Kneens—

father and son. And we're glad that our daughter is going to marry young Rod.'

7

Lavinia was plainly displeased with me when we met at Stretton-le-Soke Station and I for my part intended to challenge her about her father's statement regarding marriage to Rod. The coldness was to some extent mutual, but the idea of its lasting all the way to St. Pancras was ridiculous.

The train was not full, though it might acquire more passengers when we stopped at Derby. Meanwhile we had a compartment to ourselves. She looked at me and said suddenly:

'Why did you have to bring up the subject of Bat? Really, Jake! I thought you would have had more sense than that!'

'I was interested seeing that photo.'

'*Interested*!' The bitterness of her tone shocked me. 'You treat my family as if we were so many specimens under a microscope!'

'I never intended—'

'All right! You intended nothing. Surely your common sense should have told you that so far as possible Bat is kept out of the conversation whenever my mother is present?'

'I realised—when it was too late.'

She sighed, no longer angry with me. 'You couldn't know. That's true ... Trying to make them alter the T.T. course became an *idée fixe* with her. She wrote to the various cycling papers, long, rambling letters. She contacted a sports association—I forget the name of it now—and the Manx Motor Cycle Club. She tried her luck with the Highways and Transport Board of the Tynwald—there are nine separate boards, you know.' I nodded: 'When none of this brought forth results she approached the Lieutenant Governor himself.'

Advocate Kneen senior had warned Gabrielle of the uselessness of these tactics.

'Nothing short of a huge public outcry would cause consideration to be taken of such a request. Let's face it, Jake. A good many horses have come to grief at Beecher's Brook, but the jump wasn't removed from the Aintree course as a result.'

'I had an idea that it had been modified.'

She gave me a slight smile. Did I not realise that in England it was far easier to accomplish things when the suffering of animals rather than humans was involved?

'No comment!'·

'When the campaign failed Mother seemed to lose heart in everything. Dad was wonderful. No man could have shown greater patience and devotion.'

She told how her mother had hoarded every little possession of Bat's, refusing to destroy so much as a letter or a school exercise book that had been his. If the family had not left Douglas she would still have maintained his bedroom as a shrine. The twins had shared a room up till their school-leaving, then readjustments were made in order that each might have his own room.

Vinia paused, then:

'It's my belief she half resents Nat being still alive.'

'Surely not!'

'If one of them had to die, she would have rather it had been he.'

'Poor Nat. What quality was it that Bat had to make you regard him as you all do?'

'I can only repeat, just *being* Bat.'

She did say that she believed that her father alone of them really appreciated Nat's worth as a human being.

'Nat's put up with a lot, you know, Jake. He's such an uncomplaining sort of person. In character I suppose he takes more after the Quayle side of the family.'

This seemed the right moment for me to challenge her on the subject of marriage to Rod Kneen. What had her father meant by implying that it was 'a foregone conclusion'? Vinia avoided my glance, saying that her parents indeed took it for granted. They liked Rod and would welcome him as a son-in-law.

'To hell with that for a reason!'

My outburst seemed to amuse rather than alarm her.

'Dear Jake! You're so sweetly vehement whenever Rod's name crops up! Whatever I may decide *finally*, it will be my own decision and nobody else's. This was no time to go upsetting things further by saying that I hadn't quite made up my mind about Rod.'

'Ah! So you haven't done anything irrevocable yet?'

'No, Jake, but I shan't be able to keep him dangling much longer.'

'Cut the rope,' was my tart advice and for the first time that day she giggled.

The train slid into Derby Station and our time of privacy passed. The rest of the journey proved crowded, with a small, sticky-fingered child climbing about the carriage.

'*Aimez vous cette enfant?*' Vinia whispered, her eyes full of merriment.

'*Non!*'

We reached St. Pancras at an awkward time and she agreed to my suggestion of having a meal at the hotel. I pointed out that her flat companions might not have catered for her return and my Mrs. Trappet did not supply meals other than breakfast. Vinia insulted me by offering to go Dutch and when I refused, snapped that I need not be 'so beastly square.'

'When I can't afford to treat you, I'll tell you so, my dear.'

She stopped arguing.

'Jake, I don't want us to see each other for a bit after this.'

'Why?'

'I have to think things out.'

'Rod Kneen?'

'Amongst other matters, yes. I wouldn't just *write* and tell
152

him. If I should decide against marrying him, I'd have to go over to Castletown and tell him so to his face.'

'Would I be allowed to come with you, Vinia?'

'I'd have to see.'

Was it simple curiosity that made me so anxious to form my own judgement of Rod Kneen? Most fiction writers are fascinated by character, those little quirks of behaviour that go to the making of a composite human being. Encouraged I said:

'One of these days I want to introduce you to *my* parents, Vinia.'

Again I was guilty of trying to push things too fast. She said that would be pointless. Since I was evidently not in the habit of 'trotting out young women for their inspection' to bring one home must lead to pointless speculations.

'Speculations, no doubt. But hardly pointless,' was my amused reply.

'No, Jake, I'm not going with you to see them. That is—not until—' she broke off in delightful confusion.

The bill paid, we cut down to the tube station, Vinia again refusing to let me see her home.

'Afraid the girls might think we're going steady?'

She made a rude face at me.

'Good-bye, Jake. And thanks for the trip.'

She had gone before I had the chance to reply.

The displeasing sight of galley proofs awaited me at Southurst Road. They were, of course, the novel I had written several months back and nothing contains less interest than a book one has completed and becomes forced to re-read for errors, mindful that every correction was expensive and all inclination to re-write, resisted. My prose seemed chill and ugly: the dialogue flat. Any excitement once felt in the plot had vanished.

There was also a long letter from home, accusing me of being lax in my correspondence. At my age the idea of sitting down to compose a weekly letter to my parents seemed absurd

153

yet I knew they missed hearing from me. Not for the first time I regretted the oversight. On this occasion the task seemed more difficult than usual. To mention the visit to Stretton without involving Vinia would be awkward and the minute I acknowledged travelling somewhere with a girl Mother would be all interest in our future prospects. Having disappointed her hopes in the past I was chary of raising them until I was more certain of Vinia's intentions.

The proof correcting was as usual an urgent task and I took the finished result down in person. The publishers hoped the book might do as well as *Hollow Trumpet Sound.*

Within the next few posts came a letter from Sir Justin Hardcastle telling me that old Dan Priddy over at Lindale had died, a fact which had occasioned quite a little local publicity for we in England regard longevity with something of reverence. He kindly enclosed the cutting.

I found myself going back in thought to our visit to the cottage, with the macabre coat hanging opposite Dan on the vacant chair which once had been occupied by his wife. I thought too of the amazing thing that was memory. How this old man had been able to recall the days when the Greathearts had lived at 'Meadow End' farm, which no longer existed. Priddy who had known Lavinia Cushing's brother-in-law and now I had established a link with her living descendant.

Well, it had been a memorable visit and some day I might use both the cottage and its owner in a book.

The other item in Sir Justin's letter was even more interesting. He had been into Grange, a journey which he took with some frequency, and there met the people from whom he had bought both his house and the Lavinia Cushing portrait. He had known already that it had turned up in a sale but wondered whether the previous owners were able to add any facts about the picture's acquisition.

I told them that a young friend of mine had been very struck with the painting.

It seemed that originally the picture had been at 'Meadow End' farm and only found its way into the market when the effects from there were sold. One imagined that Charlotte Greatheart, as she then was, had found the portrait or maybe even acquired it from the painter himself. She would have determined that whatever happened it should not find its way into the Davage family. Whether Lavinia's death had been accident or murder, the husband must have been hated by Charlotte. Doubtless the two sisters had connived together so that Lavinia's clandestine love affair might be carried on in safety, until the outraged Davage arrived in pursuit of his runaway wife. But—to quote from Sir Justin's letter:

> *They—the people in Grange—bought the picture knowing nothing about its subject. Because they are fond of art, they had it cleaned by experts, with the result as we know it today.*
>
> *I still cannot understand them parting with it, having gone to much expense though I gather it was acquired in the first place for the matter of a pound or two.*

In the absence of knowledgeable buyers or art dealers, pictures in rural sales did not as a rule command high prices especially those by an unknown artist.

More than ever I was convinced that by rights the portrait should be returned to the descendants of the Cushing family. It seemed all wrong that it should hang in the home of someone entirely unconnected with them. Not of course that I could see Lavinia Cushing in either Nat's house or his parents' flat. Neither would provide a fit setting. And yet—romantically, of course, I had begun to imagine how it might look in the home which I would one day share with Lavinia. Always supposing when the time came—if it ever did—that Sir Justin were willing to sell.

I wrote thanking him for his 'revelations', which I confessed had aroused all my former interest in 'that family.' What still provoked me was not having located a single account of the shooting. There were bound to have been eye-witnesses of one kind or another, and some sort of enquiry into the fatal accident presumably made, 1872 was not so remote that somebody alive at the time might not have written about the happening. There could be a reference in a contemporary biography or a volume of *belles lettres*. There would be books about Lancashire and the Lake District which may well have included mention of the affair. The trouble was the time such a search could take—time which I had no right to devote to it. Having reluctantly dismissed the idea of personal research, I recalled that there were professionals who did this sort of work and wondered idly what they charged.

'Next time I come across an advertisement I might just enquire.'

A researcher was found and this seems as good a point as any to sketch in the result of the investigations. They were obtained from a variety of sources. Sir Francis Davage had been arrested by the Lancashire County Constabulary and brought to trial on the charge of manslaughter. His own story was that the pistol had gone off accidentally. At the most he had intended to frighten his wife. They had struggled and the pistol had discharged the bullet which mortally wounded her. As there had been no eye-witnesses—or none who came forward to give evidence—the case rested upon his uncorroborated word. The impression that he made upon the Court must have been favourable and his version of the struggle accepted. He had served a short term in prison instead of facing capital punishment. On his release he had returned to London and later married a second cousin, by whom he had a son. The family line of the Davages was not, therefore, extinct.

There was nothing further that I could learn—or indeed wished to learn—about the Davages.

The rest of the information concerned the artist Ambrose Keeling who left England shortly after the Davage trial. The young man would have stayed to find out what happened to Lavinia's husband whom Keeling surely must have regarded as murderer of his beloved. The artist had settled in Paris and died there, of tuberculosis, in his mid-forties. One gathered that his life had been one of penury relieved, perhaps, by the very occasional sale of some picture. According to an art critic discussing the 1870's—to the turn of the century in Paris, Ambrose Keeling's contributions had been small. To quote:

His work was altogether too English in style. He was undoubtedly best at portraiture. It is understood that this young man's life had been blighted by a love affair from which he had fled, upon the death of his mistress. It is quite probable that she had been his chief source of inspiration.

It did not seem worth passing any of this on to Vinia, who never had shared my interest in her ancestor. A little sadly, therefore, I wrote a note of thanks to the researcher and enclosed the cheque for these services.

I did forward the material to Sir Justin, who was gracious enough to find it 'most interesting'. In acknowledging the carbon copy he expressed the hope that I was 'now satisfied'.

Satisfied? Hardly, but at least the story had been tidied up a little and a few extra facts added to what was all that I was ever likely to learn about 'the Cushing Affair'.

8

Vinia had expressed a wish for us not to meet 'for a bit'. Since no time limit had been imposed by her and it was at least three weeks since the trip to Stretton-le-Soke, I decided to telephone.

'Jake?' her tone was doubtful yet at the same time pleased. Obviously if our love affair was to progress, the initiative must be mine.

'Hitler wasn't the only man to have his patience exhausted,' I announced in bracing tones. 'So when are we seeing one another?'

'Surely we agreed not to for the present?'

'Only under duress, so far as I was concerned. Do you want to go through life as the girl who couldn't make up her mind?'

She complained that I was 'being beastly'. So far so good! In precisely the same firm manner I reminded her that the several weeks which had elapsed ought to be enough for cogitation.

'What an authorly word to use!'

'Authorly or not, *when* and *where*?'

She said she was not sure that she liked me in my present mood. I replied, 'that was unfortunate since the mood was likely to persist until she gave me the right answer to my proposal of marriage.'

There was a long silence during which the 2d's of the S.T.D. measurements must have been ticking up madly. She gave a tremendous sigh and said that she was very busy that week. Putting in overtime at the Travel Agency.

'Paid, I trust?'

'Oh, yes.'

That meant leaving it until the weekend. Shopping on Saturday morning I was prepared to pass. The girls were having friends in for the evening.

'Theirs or yours?'

'Don't be tiresome, Jake. Well, I suppose theirs.'

'In which case there is no need for you to be in. In fact they may even prefer you to be out! I'll call for you at six o'clock and we'll have a meal somewhere.'

'Very well.' She did not sound enthusiastic.

In response to my enquiry as to whether there were a good restaurant in her district she said the Verona Trattoria was not bad.

'We'll go there then. Au revoir until Saturday.'

The rest of the week seemed to pass with maddening slowness, though there was plenty of my writing work to be done.

Also an interview with my Hall Caine publishers who sounded me out upon the idea of a further book: of the same type. I refused to touch Marie Corelli. Thomas Love Peacock, who would have interested me, had been the subject of at least one recent biography. Choice pointed to a serious assessment either of Sheridan le Fanu (the Irish descendant of the great Richard Brinsley Sheridan,) Bulwer Lytton or John Richard Jefferies 'the prose poet of rural England'. My argument against him was that his life was known to have been uneventful. If we wanted to deal with writers on vagrancy, surely George Borrow was the one to select?

Saturday dragged until such time as I could travel to Vinia's quarter of London to arrive, a trifle self-consciously, with wrapped flowers in hand. Bunty opened to me. Party or no, she was dressed as on the previous occasion.

'Oh, hello Jake. You'll find us in a bit of a state. Usually are, when we're expecting visitors. I think Lavinia's somewhere near ready.'

In actual fact she was not. I found her in the kitchen rolling brandy-snaps off a greased baking tin with agonised concentration. Gently I kissed her cheek. She flashed a false smile, promised 'not to be a tick' and proceeded to dollop out a fresh selection of gooey-mix.

'*Must* you, darling?'

'Last batch, Jake.' The oven shut, she turned, expressing pleased surprise at the flowers which I had placed upon the table. How had I known they were her 'absolute favourites'?

(I had not: but let that pass.) Before she could start a fresh chore I took her quietly but firmly into my arms.

A sudden smell from the oven made her frenzied. The brandy snaps—Father always called them jumbles—were burnt.

'We won't have to eat them, so why worry?'

'Don't be so callous, Jake.' She pulled out the tin, looking anxious. Did I think them *very* black?

'Just nicely done, my sweet.'

159

They were a good deal darker than the other array of crisp cornets, but she rolled them off and onto a cake tray without further comment. Within five minutes her coat was on and we were outside the building. I slipped my arm through hers.

The Trattoria was about six blocks away and, apart from being underlit, adequate for our requirements. An understanding waiter conducted us to a pleasantly secluded table. Massive menus were placed before us. Vinia told me that they did a good veal dish, with wine sauce. This we had to follow prawn cocktails. In such a place no sweet was an improvement upon *casata* ice-cream. Neither of us cared for Chianti, which the waiter probably deplored, and settled instead upon a lightish white wine.

During the meal I tried to put into words what I was coming to realise with every day that passed: namely that the bachelor years had gone on too long. Any man needed a home: not that of his parents but one of his own choosing. Life at Mrs. T's always had a feeling of impermanence, however long people remained there.

'You could have shared a flat with one of your author buddies,' Vinia stated in calm tones.

On the whole we were inclined to be an ivory tower set and I could not offhand think of any male friends whom I would willingly have put to the test of flat-sharing.

'You're just lazy, Jake,' giving me a mocking glance as she tasted the wine.

Quickly I passed on to the subject of meals: how tired one grew of restaurants. How much nicer it would be having all of them at home. At Mrs. T's there was a limitation to what one could cook for oneself.

'This is all very moving, I'm sure,' she answered crisply and had there been light enough to see such details, I am sure I should have found her blue eyes amused. Determined to be practical and not romantic, she said that she understood there were catering firms who delivered cooked meals.

'On wheels, you mean?'

'No, stupid. You're not old enough for those!'

'That's something!'

'I was thinking of a service we've used once or twice. You ring up and they bring a piping hot dinner to the door in containers. It isn't exactly cheap—'

'I bet it isn't!'

'Of course more often we patronise the fish and chip shop.'

In this mood Vinia was a merry person. Light-hearted in argument and skilful, too, at keeping me off any seriousness. If that was how she wanted it played— 'Do you really enjoy living with three other girls?'

'It works well enough. We have our feminine squabbles, as I suppose you'd term them. As long as nobody pinches someone else's boy friend, there are no serious quarrels.'

'And wouldn't you prefer a home of your own, Vinia?'

'Of course! Any girl wants that! If London rents weren't so expensive I should have a flat all to myself, even if it was just a combined room. But I can't afford it. Ergo—I share.'

The financial advantages, as she revealed them were obvious.

The topic seemed to have exhausted itself and the things I had meant to say went unstated. 'Well what have you been doing with yourself lately, Jake?' was an obvious lead in a different direction.

Presently she opened her bag to find a handkerchief, gave a little cry of recollection and took out a photograph.

'Mother was doing some tidying-up at home and as you seemed so interested in our family, thought you might like to see this.'

'Who is it?' peering hard and finally managing to tilt the wine-red shade so as to see.

'Grandma Arabella, of course.'

'Why yes! It would be!' The photo was a sepia print, faded from age. The young woman must have been taken a little before the turn of the century, judging by the high-necked dress and cut of the sleeves. She must have been in about her mid twenties, at the time, but looked older.

F—TB

'The date's on the back,' Vinia pointed out.

So it was! 1897. Arabella would have been two and twenty. The photographer was a Ramsey one so it had possibly been taken at the behest of her husband-to-be.

Arabella was dark, almost Spanish looking, with a full-lipped mouth, straight nose and excellently shaped brows. She stared straight ahead into the camera and looked about as happy as if she were facing a firing squad.

'She forgot to say "cheese",' I commented, passing the photo back with a smile.

Vinia held it in her hands a moment, saying: 'I wish I had known Grandma. She seemed to have had such a sad life.'

'Yes, indeed. Even in this photo hers isn't what one could call a happy face.'

'Do you think I'm like her at all, Jake?'

'Not so far as one can judge. No, my dear, you're a complete throw-back—I use the word in its nicest sense, mind!—to Lavinia Cushing. Odd in one way, since you're descended from her sister's branch of the family.'

'Perhaps Lavinia and—Charlotte, wasn't it?—were pretty alike.'

'That's something we'll never know. Ambrose Keeling evidently didn't waste paint on Charlotte and it was a bit early for photography.'

'Used they not to have things called Daguerreotypes?'

Looking it up later I found that whilst the principle of the chemical effects of light had been known as early as the 16th century, serious study had not begun until the 18th, culminating in the Wedgewood and Davy experiments of 1802. The daguerreotype plate appeared in 1839, but it was the 1850's before the wet-plate process materialised and an actual photographic society of London founded (1852). Various processes emerged between the 70's and 80's. It was highly improbable that a farming family living in Leven would have been photographed.

'Family photos are strangely unreal I always think. Are there some nice ones of you, Jake, lying around starko on a rug or in a sailor suit?'

'I'm not sure I'd show you the starko one, as you call it, and I never wore a sailor suit.'

'Oh.'

'Scout knickers and khaki shirt, that was me.'

She laughed, returned Arabella to the handbag.

The question was what to do after we left the Trattoria. Vinia's suggestion of joining the party at the flat did not appeal. Finally we went into a cinema.

It was an old picturehouse showing even older films. I was certain we had both seen this particular one before and the story seemed to develop at a much slower speed than more recent films. The setting looked to me vaguely Cornish though Vinia pointed out it was equally similar to the Isle of Man. As we were walking back to the flat, I asked whether the island was the place she wished to settle.

'Not particularly. Why?'

'I thought you were fond of it.'

'Oh, I am, Jake. After all I was born there and I spent my childhood in the place. These things count. But I've been in London several years now and I've grown to like the way of life. Everybody doesn't know everybody else.'

'That's true.'

'The seaside's quite a different place in the winter. In summer we may become a bit swamped by visitors and one's pet beachs are apt to be occupied by holiday makers instead of being nicely deserted, but at least the place is *alive.*'

'Whereas in winter it's dead?'

'Precisely. The boarding house and hotel people take their holidays. The rest of the time they repair the ravages of the previous season. Do up this room: put another wash-basin in that. The dull social events like the whist drives go on, but there isn't much left for the young people to enjoy. The summer shows are off and certain other places become shut for the winter. The fishing fleet go out, of course. And occasionally

163

one or other of the lifeboats. That's about all the excitement.'

'What's the weather like?'

'Can be blustery. On the whole I'd say it's less cold than on the mainland. The mean winter temperature is reckoned to be higher here in the south (Cornwall excepted) though in summer we actually have it somewhat cooler than you.'

'You'd have to live over there if you married Rod Kneen. You wouldn't have much option, would you? If you marry *me*, we could settle almost any place you care to choose. One great advantage about being a writer is that you can take your work with you.'

She was silent a while then told me that 'dangling sugar plums' would not cause her to depart from any decision she might have made.

'And *have* you made one, Lavinia?' I used her full name intentionally and had hold of her arm. She squirmed.

'No.'

There was no one much around and though she protested, I drew her into a doorway. We could hardly have this thing out over at the flat with a party going on. Once again I told her that I loved her and wanted us to marry and even went so far as to believe my love returned. She bit her lip but remained obstinately silent, hands thrust into her coat pockets. Except that her chin was down, instead of up, she looked more than ever like Lavinia Cushing.

'You do love me, don't you?'

'Yes, Jake!'

So she had acknowledged it at last.

'And you promise that you'll marry me?'

'I suppose so. But are you sure you really want me, Jake? I mean, what about the curse of the Cushings?'

'Darling, I'll take you, *hubris* and all.' and I pulled her to me and kissed her.

It never occurred to either of us, as I said this, in such a happy joking spirit, that there might be something in the words. That the vein of tragedy which had run through the family might not have been exhausted!

9

An unexpected commission to do some articles for one of the more learned periodicals kept me hard at my desk over the succeeding days. As usual there was a dateline and that too close for comfort.

A letter from my mother suggesting a visit from me was overdue went unanswered until the first article had gone off, when I sat down, somewhat guiltily, to apologise for the delay. (One's parents were still apt to think some dire disease or lurid experience were happening if letters were not received at reasonable intervals.) Since becoming a writer instead of a schoolmaster I regret to say that 'the gentle art of letter writing' had grown into a bore. The business ones were answered promptly because they had to be. Others less urgent lay around until I ran out of self-excuses and attended to them belatedly. To say 'I have been busy doing articles' sounded a far flimsier excuse than 'the school play is next week' or 'I'm coaching Smith Minor for his 'O' levels'!

Mother may have had to wait for her letter but I would make it up by mentioning the possibility that at long last I might be 'about to settle down'. They knew of Vinia's existence but not how she looked and somehow describing her was not easy:

She's a redhead and I think very beautiful. Her hair is not carrotty; more auburn. The sort of thing you find in paintings of Titian and Burne Jones.

Odd how painting seemed so bound up, in my own mind,

with Vinia. Yet it was not really odd at all, since it was as a painting I first had seen her ...

Mother's joyous letter came back almost by return.

You can't think how happy this news makes us both, Jake darling. I've always hated the idea of your going on living in digs, however nice you may tell me they are ... Every man needs a wife....

There was quite a lot more in that strain, then:

Couldn't you send us a photograph of Miss Quayle?

This jolted me into realisation that I did not even possess a snapshot of Vinia. To be truthful, neither had she a snapshot of me. I was not given to going around with a camera at the ready. That I had taken one to the Isle of Man was purely to find subjects that could be put to use in the Hall Caine book. I had no camera when I went out with Vinia.

Promising mother to see what could be done about a photo, I telephoned Vinia that same evening, apologising for my neglect because of the articles. She sounded slightly amused which, from anyone else, would have hipped me.

'Poor hardworking Jake!'

I cut in, saying how pleased my parents were to know about us.

'You've told them?' Her surprise was evident.

'Is there any reason in the world why I should refrain?'

After a longish pause she answered, 'No, I suppose not.'

'You wouldn't have a photo of yourself, darling, that I could send my devoted parents?'

She recollected that Nat had a film with some of her upon it.

'I'll ask him to send a snap, Jake.'

'Must you restrict it to just *one*? I'd rather like a photo for myself. And when can we see one another next?'

'As a matter of fact you aren't the only person who's been busy. At the office we're coping with the Summer tourists and at the same time compiling our brochure for next year. However—lunch together, if you like.'

'Of course I like!'

'It'll have to be within walking distance of the office, Jake. I can't take more than an hour.'

'I'll collect you at the Tourist Place and I think I know where we can be served quickly.'

'The restaurants in the stores are hopeless. I know, because I've tried them. And most of the places like the Kardomah are crowded.'

Dear Vinia! Thinking in terms of tea-shops and cafés! I could do a little better than that, as she readily agreed when I steered her into Bogatare's, which was near Vigo Street.

'Two sir?' The Greek waiter's face had a leer which I did not appreciate. Did he imagine Vinia to be a pick-up or an office popsy of mine? Coldly I told him that we were pushed for time.

'Everyone ees,' pulling out the chair for Vinia to be seated. Her warm smile soon put him in somewhat better mood. When he had gone to fetch a menu, which ideally should have been on the table, she said:

'You were pretty terse with him, Jake. Why?'

'I didn't like his manner, that's all.'

'I saw nothing wrong with it and his feet are probably killing him. They say walking on carpet is the worst.'

'Up the workers!'

'Jake, whatever's the matter?'

'Nothing! Why are we quarrelling about some wretched waiter?'

Quickly she asked about the articles I had been doing.

'You didn't tell me you went in for this sort of thing as well as books.'

'I don't as a rule. Oh, when I was schoolmastering I did a bit for the *Journal of Education* and other teaching papers, but I never claim to be a journalist or to have any training.'

'How does one train to become a writer?' she was regarding

me, chin cupped in her hands, elbow on the table, the finished melon awaiting tardy removal.

'I don't think one does "train" exactly. Mostly it's a question of trial and error and learning from one's own mistakes.'

'Not attending classes in the art of writing?'

'I never went to any, I'm afraid!'

'You taught English, though, didn't you? And you have a degree.'

'I can't swear that makes me a better author than I might have been without!'

Lunch with an eye on the clock and a certainty that service might have been quicker was not conducive to relaxation. However it was the best that could be managed. Vinia mentioned that she was doing some decorating over at the flat and my offers of help were politely rejected. I was made to feel that the four girls knew what they wanted done and were capable of carrying it out unassisted by males.

'What an independent lot you are,' I teased.

'It isn't that I don't want to see you, Jake, but you're busy and so am I. Besides I've a number of things to clear up before I go on holiday.'

'Holiday? Haven't you had one?'

'A week's leave before Easter and the long weekend over on the island, when we met.'

Stretton-le-Soke evidently did not merit inclusion.

'When are you going? And where?'

She side-stepped the direct answer very neatly indeed.

'It's just for a week—I couldn't possibly wangle more. This is our busy time. In fact they aren't pleased with me for taking a break in the high season, despite the extra hours I've put in to catch up with work.' She was talking hurriedly, afraid perhaps of being late back, yet I had no compunction about detaining her.

'You still haven't told me when—'

'Next week, Jake. It's Ramsey Bay Regatta and I've always "crewed" for Rod Kneen on board the *Lavinia*.'

I stared at her in disbelief. She was going to *crew for Kneen*? Surely in the circumstances—There was momentary distress in her eyes as she confessed that she had not told him about us, reminding me that she had to do it in person and not by post.

'I know all that,' I interrupted, 'but that hardly explains the Regatta commitment.'

'I think it does, Jake.' Dear God, how serious she looked. 'I owe as much to Rod.'

'I still don't see it that way.'

'No?'

'No!'

Once Vinia set her mind upon a course of action no one could make her change it for something different. If she had decided to crew for this man, then crew for him she would and nothing I could say would stop her. I cannot pretend that I liked the idea. She was aware of this and I sensed mutiny in her so, as the waiter placed the inevitable espresso coffee before us, I said—pleasantly as I could—that I was at a great disadvantage knowing nothing whatever about yachting.

'I've a vague idea what a catamaran looks like and that people seem to lie almost in the water—'

She laughed and called me a delightful ignoramus.

'It's a wonderful sport. Next to ski-ing, I'd think probably the most wonderful there is.'

'What exactly does crewing involve?'

'Look, Jake, I'm not a novice. I've done a lot of sailing. Not only with Rod. Don't look so sceptical.'

'Did I? Sorry!'

'The *Lavinia*'s a very good boat. It's what's called a National Twelve. The biggest competitor in the same class is, of course, the Firefly.'

'You don't say!' offering her a cigarette.

She glanced at her watch and decided there was long enough to smoke.

'There isn't time—here and now—to give you a short lecture on yachting for the beginner. How to choose your boat.

The names of the sails. What to have in the ditty box and so forth,' her amusement was obvious and the expertise in her manner impressive.

'What happens in a race exactly?'

She said that this depended upon the type of contest.

'There can be what are called Pursuit Races, where boats are handicapped. They start at different intervals but have to end up level. There are yacht team races, around bhoys: Dinghy races normally cover a course of five to ten miles, but Cruisers run over larger courses. Then there might be a one design race. This means that the entries are restricted to a specific class of boat.'

'Such as catamarans only?'

'Could be.'

'Or—what was it you called Kneen's craft again, National Twelves.'

'You're coming along nicely, Jake! There are a number of variations in handicap races. Possibly they're not quite so interesting from the spectators' point of view.'

In my mind's eye I could visualise regattas watched idly and without knowledge of what was happening, during holidays. It seemed to me that the boats often looked becalmed, so slow did their progress appear from shore. However I was willing to believe that all manner of intricate manoeuvres were being handled by the experienced helmsmen.

'Someone fires a pistol and off you all go. Right?'

'Guns, Jake, or possibly horn tootles. Ten minutes before things are due to commence there's the preparatory signal, the second gun, called the Five Minute Gun, going exactly five minutes later. From then onwards you're "under rules".'

'Ah! Like starter's orders at the Derby?'

'Pretty well the same. You must have your boat afloat and not be still on shore attending to its rigging. Oh, and the class flag—which defines the type of boat competing is broken when the ten minute gun sounds. On the five minute one they fly

170

the Blue Peter. Both flags are lowered directly the starting gun is fired.'

'On the off—if that's the right term—are the boats lined up in readiness?'

Vinia explained that their bows had to be in position to cross the line, which was of course imaginary. Either it was indicated by two floating buoys or a pair of posts ashore.

'If you cross before the starting gun, you are recalled by a further gun. In fact there could be what is termed a "general recall". And once you're off, it's usual to begin the race with a beat to windward.'

'Tell me about this Ramsey fixture.' Still slightly amused but at the same time, I suspected, gratified at finding a subject over which she was complete mistress, she said that at the Ramsey Bay Regatta races were sailed normally on handicap.

'Over an olympic-type course.'

Craft started together. Results were worked out from 'elapsed time to corrected time on handicap. Are you still with me, darling?'

One just had to say 'yes'.

'Generally speaking there are two, three or even four races, depending upon the number of dinghies of any one type competing. Perhaps Class I might be all dinghies—a handicap, the second race say Enterprise Class only and so forth.'

During the year the Manx Sailing and Cruising Club organised a number of events—though the single fixture of the Douglas and Garwick Bay Regattas was not one of them. They were, however, responsible for an off-shore race (in the cruiser section) round the Isle of Man and certain interport contests for which there were various trophies. Rod Kneen had competed in most races over the years and had won quite a few cups.

'But never the Ellan Vannin Challenge Trophy for which we are competing this year—' She broke off to exclaim in dismay:

'Jake! The time!'

I summoned the waiter, paid the bill and accompanied her back to the travel bureau. Through the glass doors queues of people could be seen browsing at brochures and talking to counter clerks. Vinia gave me a hurried kiss and disappeared inside these doors.

I began to saunter up towards Oxford Circus, still mildly troubled about this business of Vinia and Rod Kneen. What little she had been able to tell me about the sailing (between gulps of coffee and puffs at her cigarette) had not been all that helpful. I still did not know whether Kneen were a good or a bad yachtsman and what sort of a chance he had in the Regatta; with his National Twelve. However since he was an islander I suppose that I should accept his competence and, since Vinia had sailed with him often before, the likelihood that between them they would know what they were about in any race.

It was not the race so much as an ethical question that troubled me. By going with Kneen was she being disloyal to me?

'She loves yachting and he has one. Point number two—and I'm not sure just how important this really is—there happens to be the friendship which he (and his father) have shown to her family.'

Vinia was aware that the young man hoped, expected even, to marry her. Surely it was no kindness on her part to crew for him and at the end of the race say:

'Sorry, Rod, but we aren't going to be married after all because I've met someone I like better.'

Not that one could imagine Vinia putting it quite so bluntly as that. In order to deliver this message it seemed totally unnecessary for her to rush to Ramsey and don those bright yellow oilskins that people wore when they went yachting simply because she had crewed for Rod Kneen in other years. Even her passionate invocation on yachting as a sport could not justify this step. If she were that mad on boats surely there were clubs she could join? And why not spend her holiday on the Broads or down at Bosham, that most delightful creek in Chichester harbour.

It was my secret belief that Vinia was not just unwilling to tell Rod Kneen of her decision not to marry him but actually *afraid* to do so.

10

There were a number of reasons why I decided to visit the Isle of Man again but the motives did not bear floodlighting. In the first place, of course, there was a natural—maybe even a forgivable—curiosity regarding Rod Kneen. What sort of a man was he? It was inconceivable that I should not manage to meet him.

There was also the matter of Vinia herself. It was not that I had any doubts about her love for me. I had long since accepted this in all humility and gratefulness. Neither did I doubt her promise to tell young Kneen about us. What I did fear, was the extent to which she might find herself swayed by him.

At first the idea of her going off to crew for him had made me angry. Surely there must be something she and I might have done together instead? I did not believe yachting to be an obsession with her.

Maybe nothing was more natural than that she should desire to spend what little leave she had in the familiar Manx territory: the dear 'Ellen Vannin' of song and fable. Just as one supposed rally drivers were unable to resist entering year after year for such events as the Monte, once one had raced in a yacht several times in an annual regatta, probably there was the same urge to continue competing. Kneen had never won that particular trophy. And this year conditions might seem

173

especially favourable. So much for my reasons for wanting to go. I should have contacted the Isle of Man Yacht Club for details. As it was I confused the date of the Ramsey Bay Regatta and missed seeing the race in which the *Lavinia* competed.

I underestimated the advance bookings for August. All seats on the planes to the island were fully bespoken. This meant switching to British rail and steamer, an infinitely slower form of travel. The overnight journey to Liverpool was tedious to say the least and once there, a case of queueing for the 10.30 ship which was not, I found, the *Manx Maid* car ferry steamer but one of the passenger service ones doing the Liverpool-Douglas run. Everywhere on board was packed. Families crowded together, sitting, standing or leaning against whatever was handiest. Liverpudlian youths, long haired and transistor-set equipped, moved around in groups, sometimes accompanied by girl friends, sometimes not. Children ran, restless and full of screams. Cups of tea were slopped around and sandwiches munched wherever there was space to sit.

Going down the Mersey one was too busy trying to find a resting place of some kind and open sea followed for the next long spell. It might have been rewarding to watch the approach to landfall, were it not that this time we were all madly queueing again to leave the ship. All in all it was a monotonous three and three quarter hours afloat!

It was my intention to stay in Douglas only for a meal and to phone one or two Ramsey hotels. They were: booked up. Where I had stayed before they were regretful, but thought it unlikely that I should find anywhere local. They suggested an hotel just outside the town at Sulby—between the Glen and the Bridge. This time I struck lucky.

Having tidied myself and made some enquiries about the Regatta, only to find that it was all over, I wondered what to do and decided to try the hotel where Vinia would be staying. I found her in the bar—Manx licensing hours did not follow those on the mainland—with a man whom I guessed must be Rod Kneen.

'Surprise! Surprise!' she exclaimed, swinging herself off the stool. 'I had a feeling you might turn up, Jake. Rod—this is Jake Wickham.'

Kneen proved taller than I had expected from his somewhat crouched attitude at the bar counter. He was one of those dark, saturnine people with a good figure for his age, which I took to be about forty: he was older than I had assumed. His eyes were deepset with hooded lids; his mouth firm. The lips I thought a little too thin. Not, one would have said, the sort of man to make an immediate hit with women. He was informally dressed in sharkskin trousers, sports shirt with a blue neck scarf and blazer bearing an Isle of Man Yacht Club badge on the pocket.

We eyed one another warily, as men do who happen to want the same woman. Vinia merely looked anxious. To break the tension I asked how the race had gone. Immediately Rod's face became animated. He spoke in rather a precise sort of way, smiling indulgently each time Vinia chipped in with some comment. It was to be gathered that the race in question had been of the handicap variety.

'The lower the handicap number, the faster the boat. An eighty-seven rating has to gain seven minutes on one rated ninety-four.'

'In how long a time?'

'One and a half hour's sailing. Look, Wickham, let me explain the course.' He did—at some length. I gathered that from the start at A, the first lap to B was what was called a Reach (wind coming across the hull) as was the section B to C. Then they changed to a Beat; (wind dead ahead) from C back to A.

'One has to tack,' and he indicated pencil lines on his sketch. 'The second lap is a Run, wind directly behind. The third lap is same as the first, the fourth as the second lap.'

Vinia caught my eye and winked. Kneen's commentary went on, recapturing the triumph, lap by lap. Only half listening to the technicalities which it was doubtless impossible to avoid, I

175

caught some reference to being 'the third boat', lying third in the race, I assumed. Remembering the old island superstition I asked whether third boats were not supposed to be unlucky.

'Or does that only mean the third boat out of harbour?'

For a second he looked genuinely puzzled then smiled: 'Ah! You must be thinking of the fishing fleet. As you say, I believe there used to be quite a firm belief that the third boat to leave harbour might prove unlucky. I wouldn't say they think about it much at the present day. Though I must confess that some superstitions die hard—especially in island communities.'

'Anyway I take it you didn't have any ill luck?'

'On the contrary,' this was Vinia speaking. 'We did most frightfully well and carried off the trophy!'

I hope that I made suitable congratulatory sounds.

'What's your poison, Wickham?' beckoning the bar tender.

'Please! Let me! Vinia? Gin and something?' and allowing no quarter I stood the round. Talk was very general over the drinks. Vinia seemed unsure of herself in a way I had not seen before: as if she half expected me to be angry with her. I hope that I managed to convey that I was not. As for Rod Kneen, I neither liked nor disliked him. He struck me as a competent character with a superficial line in pleasantry. He gave no hint of resenting my presence: in fact went out of his way to express regret that he and Vinia were booked up for that evening. It seemed that they were going to a party in celebration of their victory. If they had known—hastily I said that I intended to look up my friend, Miss Quinn.

'Have you done any yachting yourself, Wickham?' he asked over the next round of drinks.

'Afraid not.'

Did Vinia think that I would like to come on a trip? Immediately she grabbed my arm and said it would be a wonderful idea.

'She's a lovely craft, Jake.'

'Named after you she'd better be!' (Did I detect a gleam of

annoyance in Kneen's eyes at this remark?) Be that as it might he was offering to take me out next day for a sail right round the island. Lavinia caught his eye questioningly and he smiled.

'I wasn't suggesting we did it in my boat.' Turning to me he explained that sailing round Man entailed a minimum of 80 miles. Too much for a dinghy to attempt in the ordinary way. In any case three people aboard a National 12 would be quite cramped and there would be no possibility of preparing a meal. 'You wouldn't want us to starve, now would you, Wickham?' He added that such a sail would be a delightful experience. There were bays and rock formations that could be seen so much better from the water.

'It's very kind of you, but isn't it going to be a lot of bother? Borrowing a craft, and all that?'

Kneen laughed, saying there would be no difficulty. Then addressing Vinia rather than me said a small cruiser would serve the purpose. An Eventide, Debutante or Folkboat, all three types were owned locally.

'Old Hickson's Eventide would be just the job, wouldn't it?'

I laughed and said that my experience so far had been one trip round the Calf.

'Ah yes!' he said, dismissing this as rather a touristy attraction as compared to island-viewing from the deck of a cruiser. He promised however to produce an extra Mae West lifejacket and a set of oilskins in case the weather turned out rough. Was I a good sailor? Modesty made me claim to be average.

'You'll have no time to be seasick, will he Rod?' heartless Vinia laughed.

'No doubt I'll be too busy dodging the boom, or whatever you call it!'

We made the arrangements for meeting next day and I offered to bring a share of food. Or would we be too busy to eat?

'Not on your sweet life,' Kneen assured me, saying with a long, deep look at Vinia, that she was highly skilled at knocking up a meal under any weather conditions.

'The met. report this morning was pretty fair. So long, Wickham. Be seeing you!' and he turned once more to his companion.

Was I piqued? Well, just a little, though I hardly knew what more I had expected. Vinia to rush into my arms on sight? She had always been shy of public demonstrations of affection and to have behaved in such a way in front of Kneen would have been hurtful to him. He had been pleasant enough. After all he had invited me for this sail. To please Vinia or to show off in a yacht?

The phone call to Miss Quinn resulted in a command to come round to coffee that evening. She seemed amused that I had let myself in for a yachting cruise round Man.

'I hope you're a good sailor, because there are plenty of cross currents.'

'Actually I am—very.'

Which effectively ended the topic.

It was just after ten when I left, aware of being suddenly very tired which was hardly surprising since I had been on the go ever since leaving London the previous day.

The morning looked fair. Realising that I had brought no suitable gear for yachting with me I had taken the precaution of buying jeans and a T shirt on my way to meet them. Espadrilles I already had being averse to using decent shoes to walk about on beaches. Add the anorak that had done service on so many holidays and I was ready for anything.

''Morning skipper!'

Rod looked up and grinned. He was wearing shorts, plimsols and a hooded anorak. 'Crew not turned up yet,' meaning Vinia. He finished whatever it was he had been doing and gave me a hand to board the cruiser. 'That's the *Lavinia* lying out there,' and he indicated a very smart looking yacht.

For sentimental reasons, I suppose, I was sorry we were not using it for this trip, however I could see that the cruiser he had borrowed was a very impressive craft and certainly more spacious.

He pointed out what various things were for and tossing me the cigarettes, gave what amounted to a cram course on what the novice had best know for his own and other's safety.

'For your guidance, Wickham, a capsize isn't as bad as it sounds and can be fairly easily overcome, if you know the drill.'

'Which you and Vinia do?'

He nodded. It depended, said he, upon wind direction. One stayed 'out of the main force' when the wind was against one and in the middle of it when it was 'with one'. If we should capsize—which he admitted *could* happen, though it was un-likely unless sudden rough conditions set in, the broad prin-ciple of the thing was as follows:

'Blown leeward, you'll go over that side. What you then do is to swim round the boat until you are amidships, as near as dammit. Never pull the boat with you as you go in. Grab the gunwale and lever hard till the boat rolls upright. Go about. Then start bailing!'

To cheer me up he mentioned that a capsize could bring the boat on top of the crew then one swam out from under and proceeded to try to right the boat. He spoke about 'Gybe' and 'tack', both of which terms meant little to me.

'In heavy weather we reef the mainsail and maybe drop the jib.'

'Are you expecting either eventuality?'

'Of course not! I was only trying to gen you up a bit. Great thing is, stay calm. Don't panic but obey orders. Lavinia and I will tell you what to do. She's jolly good for a landlubber.'

Just then she appeared, contriving to look both smart and serviceable in slacks and ancillary equipment. She carried a dufflebag which she stowed and the next few minutes were occupied with casting off from the quay, an operation which I could but watch admiringly.

The day proved far more pleasant than I had anticipated and once aboard Rod Kneen seemed to acquire a different dimension. He was calm, carefully calculating every adjust-ment to sail or steering. He issued his orders quietly. He and

Vinia worked together in an experienced fashion. For the most part I was given only the small, unimportant tasks, as befitted the complete novice.

She came and sat with me for a while while he was at the other end of the cruiser. We spoke together in low voices. It was our first uninterrupted bit of conversation since my arrival.

'Have you told him?' I asked, not needing to say more.

'Yes. Last night, as a matter of fact. I wanted the race over and thought now that he'd seen you, it would be easier.'

'And was it?' feeling curious.

She shook her head. He had minded greatly? She nodded.

'I wonder he didn't call this trip off.'

'Oh, Rod would never do a thing like that!'

I was forced to admire his pleasant, relaxed manner and the fact that he was not allowing personal disappointment to spoil our day.

When he came up to us again he must have been able to tell the conversation from our faces. He sent Vinia for'ard and squatted beside me a second, taking his pipe out of his mouth to speak:

'I think I knew about things already.'

Just that—nothing else.

The day wore on and we were still aboard long after dusk, battling with a sou'westerly gale force wind which had sprung up and was making the return to Ramsey considerably harder than any of us had envisaged.

The deck was awash and slippery as an ice-rink. The three of us were wet wherever our oilskins did not touch. Vinia managed to smile gamely enough in between her duties. The sails had been trimmed for greater safety. I never realized how difficult hauling at canvas in heavy seas could be. My untrained muscles ached but I thought, amateur that I was, I had not done too badly. Then the worst wave of the lot hit us and the next thing I knew I was being flung overboard. Borne on the wind came Vinia's frantic cry of 'Jake! Jake darling!'

*   *   *

Quotation from the Royal National Life-Boat Institution report: Ramsey, Isle of Man, at 8.56 p.m.

the coastguard informed the Ramsey honorary secretary that a small cruiser appeared to be in trouble about two miles north east of Ramsey. At 9.06 p.m. the coastguard reported that the cruiser was making heavy weather and was only about 60—70 yards off the shore. The lifeboat 'Thomas Corbett' was launched on an ebbing tide at 9.22 p.m. and found the casualty in the position indicated. Despite a south westerly gale force wind and a very rough sea the lifeboat went close in shore and was able to get a line on board the cruiser and to tow her into Ramsey Harbour.

II

The fearful experience was one that I am not likely to forget and even afterwards, when the three of us were sipping hot grog in the Isle of Alanis hotel, where we had been taken, in dry clothes at last, precisely what happened was far from clear. I remembered going overboard and bobbing about in a sea too rough for swimming.

'You saved my life, Rod,' I heard myself saying in a thick voice, for my throat was sore from trying to talk above the wind and perhaps a little from the salt water I had swallowed.

As Vinia explained it all to me later; in nice, non-technical language, Rod had thrown me a rope which I had managed to catch and hold on to. The trickiest part of the whole operation had been hauling me back on board. She had held onto Rod to steady him. At any moment the pair of them might have slithered into the water or be swept in, as I had been. Clambering aboard, dragged there by strong arms, I had spread-eagled, exhausted. Vinia manoeuvred me to the cabin, and gave me brandy, her face still wet from a mixture of spray and tears. To crown everything, I passed out cold.

Rod had ordered her to stay below, preferring to run no risks for her safety. The poor chap must have cursed for not having turned about when the weather first changed, though it did so quickly ...

I recall being a bit sick—salt water mostly—and Vinia ministering to me and, rather later, shouts and hailing sounds. Rod came and told us that the lifeboat had been sent to the rescue. Truth to tell he did not look over pleased at the news. Maybe his *armour prope* as yachtsman was a bit dented?

I refused to 'skulk down below' any longer and clasping Vinia firmly by the hand, repaired on deck to the splendid sight of the red and blue boat bobbing across the water towards us. They had some difficulty manoeuvring into position to throw us the line which, redeeming myself a little, I managed to catch.

We were then towed ashore.

'You won't want to go yachting again in a hurry,' Rod said, turning to me with a weary smile. His chin had more than five o'clock shadow. He was the type to grow a heavy beard.

'Oh, I wouldn't say that exactly—'

'Lavinia, I'm sorry our last trip should have turned out as it did. I ought to have turned about. Not hung on, hoping to ride it out.' He sighed. ' "All's well that ends well", as the bard says. God, but I'm tired.'

She looked concerned. 'Why don't you go home, Rod? I'm sure we could find someone to drive you.'

At that he looked really angry. He was perfectly capable of driving himself home. Vinia was already staying in the hotel and I could take a taxi to Sulby.

'Drop you, if you like.'

'It's out of your way,' I answered, which was true and he

did not argue. 'In case I don't see you again—all the best.'

I found it in my heart to admire the apparent sincerity with which he said this. He turned to kiss Vinia briefly on one cheek, then waving, left the hotel.

'You understand now why telling him was so difficult—Jake.'

Vinia looked as if she, too, had had about enough for one day and I said that I, too, would be turning in, when a taxi had been ordered. As it happened one was passing so there was no need to hang around the hotel waiting.

'Good night, Jake,' It was a very subdued Vinia who said this.

The taxi driver seemed to have heard all about our adventure. Inevitably it would have been round Ramsey by now and on the morrow, no doubt the rest of the island.

Vinia phoned me about 10 a.m. to know how I was and to enquire if I had slept well. Apart from an unpleasant nightmare about drowning, I had, but ached in a number of muscles. She said that she had not had a very good night but would tell me about it when we met at the Alanis for lunch. As soon as I had hung up, there was another call for me: Rod Kneen wanting to be assured there were no ill effects from the adventure.

'No. I'm fine. And you?'

'Starting a head cold but otherwise O.K.'

He asked if I had heard from Vinia and I told him we were meeting for lunch. Would he not join us? He hesitated then said somewhat unconvincingly that he could not afford the time. He had a business appointment, which just might have been true.

'You go back by the four p.m. boat today, don't you?'

Again he wished me 'all the best.' While I was dressing came the third call. This time it was Miss Quinn, wanting to know 'what on earth we had been up to on the previous day.'

'Nothing much really.' Playing it down somewhat I said we had run into heavy seas and the coastguard had thought it wise to send out a rescue party.

'Yes, yes, so I gather. But which of you went overboard?'

'I did, I'm afraid. As you can hear, I'm still alive.'

She grunted and expressed the opinion that town-dwelling authors might be better advised to stick to shore activities.

'You're right, I guess.' After some further chit-chat, we said good-bye.

Vinia had been to the hairdresser and her bedraggled locks of the previous evening were restored to their natural glory. Apart from dark rings of fatigue round her eyes, she looked much as usual.

'Jake, darling,' kissing me fleetingly, for the hotel was not the most private of places. 'Are you still going home today? That's what I thought. I'm all packed up, so we can travel together.'

Over lunch she looked unwontedly serious.

'Penny for them,' I prompted, smiling across at her.

'Jake, you know the way we've talked about the curse of the Cushings? How something fatal seems to happen to descendants of the family—or the people they marry? Do you think—yesterday was part of it? That you fell overboard because *I* was on the yacht?'

I saw what she meant, only if there were anything in that theory of mine—and suddenly I wanted to disbelieve it with all my might—then surely by rights I ought to have been drowned instead of sitting having lunch with my love.

'Suppose I am right, Jake, and I've been thinking about this —most of the night, would it be at all possible that something has happened to break the bad luck? That it could be outlived or—or defeated by some power—'

'Such as?'

'Love,' she said the word almost in a whisper, then: 'Jake, what did you think about when you were in the water?'

'You, my darling. I didn't have time to be afraid over myself. All I wanted was to be back on board to make sure nothing frightful happened to you.'

She sighed in a kind of relief. 'I'm glad you said that, Jake,

184

because all the time you were struggling about in the sea I was praying harder than I've ever prayed before—' She broke off, then resumed. 'When you were back with us—looking like a half-drowned porpoise—'

'I thought porpoises were black, not yellow oilskin coloured!'

She ignored the interruption. 'I felt how very precious life was.'

'Our lives? Yes. And poor old Rod Kneen's, too. You're a lucky lass, Vinia, to have two such staunch lovers.'

'Perhaps that's the answer. Both of you being there. The Cushings—the Kermodes—they must have been different. Just one lover at a time—does this sound an awful lot of bilge, Jake?'

Faced with such an appeal it would have been ungallant to agree. Heaven knew I had every bit as much reason to want the family curse or the effects of *hubris* to be broken and said so to her.

'Let's hope it's true, darling.'

'They do say that if you believe in something strongly enough it becomes a fact.'

As the lyric of that song in Lehar's operetta *Paganini* puts it, girls 'were made to love and kiss'. Not, God bless them, for logic!

12

'You are quite right. The likeness is extraordinary,' and Sir Justin stood to one side, glancing first at the Keeling portrait and then at Vinia herself. 'If your wife were to don a similar dress for a ball—er, I don't suppose they have balls nowadays, do they?'

'Well, not very often,' and we smiled to one another in the way that newly-weds will.

'I've heard so much about this picture from Jake, Sir Justin. In fact I'm sure that he's far more in love with Lavinia Cushing than he's ever been with me.'

'What rot, darling!'

Turning to me she said: 'Well perhaps you do regard me as a sort of understudy.'

Sir Justin was a little nonplussed by all this: uncertain, perhaps, how our badinage was to be taken. Humorously? Or as a kind of half truth?

'Actually I'd say that Lavinia Cushing was much more attractive than I am. There's a—*je ne sais quoi* about her, don't you think?'

'A commanding beauty,' suggested Sir Justin, his eyes back upon this minor painter's masterpiece. 'I'm not an imaginative sort of man as a rule but to me that is the face of a typical *femme fatale*. A woman whose fatal beauty and power brings ruin and tragedy to those who come in contact with her.'

The gracious room in Cartmel was suddenly quiet. Vinia plucked at the loose button on her coat pocket, making it looser still. Our host continued to gaze steadfastly at the picture while I travelled in memory back to the day when first I had seen it and wanted above all to learn the story of the portrait and its subject. Well I had found out a great deal about the Cushings and those who came after them and now that I was married to Vinia I hoped perhaps that together we might still contrive to add to the existing knowledge. We were spending part of our honeymoon in the Lake District and it was our intention to visit the places connected with the family's past. Leven and the little village church at Urswick where Lavinia Cushing was buried; and, if it were at all possible to arrange, we would cross the sands of Morecambe Bay just as they had done in the olden times, retracing the paths which travellers had taken by coach and upon foot.

I was no longer afraid of *hubris* because it seemed that Vinia had managed to break the train of tragedy.

These thoughts flitted through my mind as the three of us

settled ourselves, waiting to be joined by 'Kate' Hardcastle, who had been out on one of her local missions when we called. Sir Justin was delighted to see us and had, of course, known that we were staying in Grange. To be truthful I had thought about making it Cartmel instead but decided it was putting us rather too close to the Hardcastle's doorstep. Also there were more places to stay in a seaside resort.

Kate bustled in, full of apologies, for we had 'phoned to ask if the hour would be convenient to both of them.

'Of course you'll stay for tea,' she exclaimed having given the order on her way to join us.

'We've been commenting upon the likeness of young Mrs. Wickham—'

'Vinia, please,' interrupted my wife. He bowed to her.

'Vinia, then, and the portrait.'

'Kate' studied the two faces then pursed her lips indecisively, saying that she supposed there was 'quite a look': especially the distinctive shade of the hair, adding, with the sensibleness one expected from her, that family resemblances were peculiar and unpredictable.

'Now take myself. If I'm like anyone at all, then it's my grandmother,' and going over to a curio table in the corner she took out a painted miniature and handed it to us in turn for inspection. She was quite right. The hair grew in the same peak upon the forehead, also there was a look about the eyes themselves and in the actual contours of the face.

Retrieving the miniature she observed:

'That is understandable, if I may say so, but the idea that your charming wife, Mr. Wickham—'

It was my turn to cut in with, 'Jake, please,' and hers to repeat the name.

'—Jake, should resemble someone so remotely connected with her is a bit difficult to credit.'

'But the likeness is there, my dear,' pointed out Sir Justin, breaking off his remarks in order to rise and open the door for their maid to bring in the great silver tray of tea things. There was all the graciousness of an early age with the cake stand containing three tiers of foodstuffs and the pouring out from Georgian silver teapot and accessories.

Before we left I asked whether they would dine with us one evening at Graythwaite Manor over at Grange. They looked half amused.

'Are you quite sure? I mean isn't this your honeymoon?'

'We would be so glad if you would both come,' Vinia spoke up without any prompting and I could tell that she liked them both.

Details were duly arranged. Outside was the two-seater Capri model, my wedding present to Vinia. (We took turns at the driving.) After all I had had to produce something showier than Rod Kneen's pale blue car!

It was next day when we were strolling along by the swimming pool and I was recounting to Vinia my bathe with the quicksands on my first visit ever to these parts. A young-middle-aged couple, about to pass, stopped abruptly and stared at us.

'Extraordinary!' she exclaimed.

'Amazing!' this was from him.

Their astonishment was too genuine to appear rude. To avoid literally barging into them we also had halted. Vinia looked enquiringly at them, then at me. Recovering first, the man apologised for their possible bad manners.

'You must think us quite, quite mad, but this young lady reminds us of someone—' he broke off in complete confusion.

'Someone we've never actually seen because, well, it wasn't possible—' the wife's rescue effort was unsuccessful but by this time I had realised who they must be. The previous owners of the Keeling portrait. I spoke up at once:

'You used to have that picture which is at present at Sir Justin Hardcastle's home in Cartmel? Right?'

'Yes we did. You know him?'

'*And* the portrait. As a matter of fact my wife—the name's Wickham, by the way,—is a descendant of Lavinia Cushing.'

Their sanity vindicated, we all decided that this chance meeting—perhaps not so chance as all that, for Grange was hardly a large resort—called for a drink. We repaired to the Grand. Their name was Paterson-Stubbs and he was an architect who had designed their present place of residence which he confessed was ultra-modern. A little too much so, in the opinion of some, for its seaside setting.

'The portrait would have looked all wrong and in any case it needed a higher wall to show it off properly. So we put it into a sale.'

'Without any reserve. After all, the artist was unknown, wasn't he?' Mrs. Paterson-Stubbs smiled at us politely in turn.

'Sir Justin did tell me he had bought it quite cheaply.'

'Almost for the proverbial song. I forget exactly how much he paid. We had several other things in the same sale and it's quite a while ago. I gather he was very pleased with his purchase and it goes splendidly in his room. They very kindly invited us round to their place,' the architect husband made this contribution.

The Paterson-Stubbs were not people we were likely to meet again and the interest in one another was, of course, a transitory one. Neither was there anything fresh to be learned from them about the portrait. He said that it had been the painting of the dress which had appealed to him in the first place and decided him to buy the picture.

'You know what country sales are like. A few good pieces and a lot of junk. The catalogue was not exactly enlightening. My wife may recall what it said about the picture. Do you, my dear?'

'Not the exact wording, Brian, but the gist of it was "Portrait of a nineteenth century lady. Miss Lavinia Cushing. By A. Keeling."'

'The artist may be unknown or practically so, but a chap who could make silk appear to *live*, as it does in the picture, had to be pretty good.' Paterson-Stubbs thought a moment, then asked whether either of us were familiar with Parham, a stately home of repute in the Storrington area. 'No? Well there's a Van Dyke there. Can't tell you who the lady is, but the dress is a miracle of brushwork.'

And he was quite right for Vinia and I made a point of visiting Parham later, when we were back in London, and Mme. Kirke's portrait was all Paterson-Stubbs claimed. In fact it would have been worth the journey just to see that and nothing else. To equate Ambrose Keeling with Van Dyke was possibly too much, still there was a touch at least of a similar genius.

Pleasant though it was drinking at the Grand there would be lunch waiting for us and Vinia suggested that we should be making a move.

'And where are you both staying?'

We told them. Fortunately their interest was no more than that of residents towards visitors. It was possible they guessed we were on our honeymoon.

'I was so afraid you'd natter on and on with them about the picture, Jake. That's why I cut in about lunch. I hope it didn't sound rude?'

'I could feel you sending out waves of S.O.S's to me, darling! I wasn't anxious either to become involved any further with them.'

'We had nothing in common, had we?'

'Only the picture, I guess.'

'You and your old picture, Jake. I'm jealous. Madly jealous of Lavinia Cushing.'

'You haven't the least reason to be, love. A flesh and blood wife's a lot better than a canvas of any woman,' which seemed to wrap up the topic neatly enough exactly as we reached Graythwaite Manor.

From Grange we went on up to my parents who had not of course met Vinia before and they took to her at once. I feel certain Mother had a lovely heart-to-heart with her, expressing all the joy that she felt to have her son married at last. Father was

190

looking in better health again, which was a great relief. All in all it was a singularly happy visit and, if I had not known this already, I would have found out how adaptable to all manner of human relationships Vinia was. She would have been as simple and friendly in the cottage of old Dan Priddy (had he still been alive) as she had been at Sir Justin's home.

Before we left Yorkshire he telephoned and asked to speak to me.

'Look, Jake, we've been talking it over and we both feel that the right place for Lavinia Cushing would be in your new home. Therefore I hope that you will accept her from us both as a wedding present.'

Hearts may not in fact leap, though there can be a physical sensation pretty near it which I experienced then. Of course I demurred out of politeness, hardly imagining any show of reluctance on my part could sound convincing. Still it had to be attempted.

'But the picture looks so splendid where it is. And you're both attached to it, Sir Justin.'

'We like it, yes, but it means something to you people whereas to us it's, well, just an attractive painting.'

'Won't it leave an awful gap?'

He chuckled and said there were always sales going on around the countryside and he had no doubt that in due course they would find something equally suitable for 'above the fireplace.'

'It's bound to leave a mark on the wall.'

'Have no fear, dear boy. Kate has already made this the excuse for having the room redecorated.'

We men could see no possible necessity for these things until a place became so shabby, perhaps, as to make us notice. Women were different with their spring cleanings and constant demands for replacements because this or that looked worn or faded. All this I knew already in theory. The in-practice part was still to come!

I could not honestly think that the Hardcastle's room needed re-doing. Places kept so much cleaner in the country. Still perhaps the satin-stripe paper was dulled? By age rather than dirt, let me hasten to state.

Sir Justin felt that to despatch the Cushing portrait by road or rail services might invite damage, even if he had it crated. He suggested that we made the necessary diversion to include Cartmel in our homeward run.

'There's no necessity for you to go to an hotel. You'd be more than welcome. You know the house and that we have two spare rooms. The single where you slept and a double.'

'I doubt if we need to put you to all that trouble, Sir Justin, but may I ring you back later?'

I must say that Vinia took the news of the picture much more calmly than I had done.

'Now you'll be happy, darling,' her tone was teasing, but her eyes shone with love.

'Won't you?'

'Oh, yes, because at least I'll have my rival under the same roof!'